NIGHTSHADE'S
REQUIEM

Other Books by Anthony Hains

NIGHTSHADE'S
REQUIEM

Nightshade Chronicles
Book 1

Anthony Hains

Nightshade's Requiem

Published by PCNY BOOKS

Cover design by Elderlemon Design
Book interior by Cover to Cover LLC

ISBN: 978-1-7323880-2-4 (Ebook)
ISBN: 978-1-7323880-3-1 (Paperback)

I worked with countless kids and teenagers as a psychologist for almost forty years. They taught me a great deal about courage, resiliency, and curiosity. This book is dedicated to them.

Contents

1   Cole Gets Taken for a Ride   1

2   The Tour Begins   13

3   Slaver and Stern and the Demons   18

4   Things Get Creepy   34

5   Warming Up the Crowd   52

6   Worst Birthday Ever   57

7   Timmy Wins H-O-R-S-E and Cole Gets Shocked   75

8   The Leaper and the Creeper   91

9   Chaz Captures Shirley Temple   103

10   Lambert Provides the Lay of the Land   113

11   Chaz Tells the Sad Stories   130

12   Kenny and the Milk Truck   134

13   What the Creeper Did   146

14   Timmy Makes a Mess   162

15   Three Boys in a Photo   174

16   Not a Good Place for Kids   184

17   Kenny's First Lobotomy   203

18   The ECT Review   219

19   The Dead Tunnel   226

20   Requiem   241

1

Cole Gets Taken
for a Ride

September 1962

THE BLOOD SEEPING DOWN THE back of his throat had slowed considerably, so that crappy taste in his mouth wasn't as bad anymore. Still, he kept getting remnants of the metallic flavor whenever he swallowed, and it was disgusting.

His reflection in the car window was hard to see because of the late-afternoon sun. Whenever the car made its way under the shade of trees lining the road, however, he could catch glimpses of his face and shock of black hair in the glass. These brief images displayed swaths of deep red smears crusted across his lips and cheeks. Even his chin had smudges that reminded him of a goatee. The crimson around his nostrils added to the effect.

All this courtesy of Bruce, his foster father.

"That'll teach you to lie," Bruce had said after knocking him to the kitchen floor for the second time. Droplets of blood sprayed the linoleum. Bruce grabbed him hard enough to practically yank off his T-shirt. It was up around his armpits, and splotches of red were rapidly spreading over the dull white.

"Just get him out of here. Damn kid gives me the creeps. His lies and his heathen rituals," Dorie screamed at her husband. She tossed a packed suitcase in the general direction of the back door where it landed with a dull thud. "For cripes' sake, Bruce, you're getting blood everywhere. Don't make me more work. Just go."

Dorie was beet red. Her eyes were blazing mad, and her piercing stare was meant to shake him to his very core. It didn't. The impact was spoiled by strands of colorless hair spiking haphazardly from pink curlers that bobbled with each word she yelled. If his mouth hadn't been hurting so much, he'd probably smile—maybe even laugh.

"You dirty little creep. Think you can do your nasty little things with Bobbi Anne and talk your stupid lies? You think you can curse this family?"

Bobbi Anne stood well behind her mother in the den off the kitchen. Her hands were clutched together with knuckles gleaming white from the pressure. Her teddy-bear eyes, naturally round and cute under normal conditions, bulged in panic. He thought they might burst out of her skull.

The car swooped unexpectedly down a lengthy hill and his stomach dropped. He usually enjoyed the sensation of feeling suspended in midair, but not now. He couldn't get his mind off the fear in Bobbi Anne's eyes.

The first time he'd seen her look so scared was when the hulking shadow materialized in Bobbi Anne's bedroom doorway and strode silently over to her bed. Bobbi Anne, unable to budge in the slightest, gaped at the approaching shadow over the bed covers. The shadow paused just a moment and tossed the covers off the girl with a snap. Bobbi Anne whimpered once, then went silent as the shadow touched her and did things to her.

He stole his way back up the stairs to his room, counting to four with each step. If there was any creak or snap of the wood, he would need to return to a lower stair and start again. He made absolutely sure this didn't happen.

Bobbi Anne was nine. Two years younger than him. No, his birthday was just around the corner. That would make him three years older.

He told his foster mother what he saw, but she didn't believe it. In fact, they thought *he* was the shadow-thing that entered Bobbi Anne's room and did the nasty things. Bobbi Anne insisted it wasn't him, but under increasingly intense pressure from both her parents, she revised her story. He was slapped again and again over the next few days. And kept locked in his room where he counted words in a book instead of reading. If he ended with an even number, he was okay and the bad things stayed behind the walls. If he ended with an odd number, then he'd have to start again. If an image of the bad things came to his mind, he'd have to think of words with an even number of letters and keep his thoughts on something pleasant like rainbows and puffy clouds. *Heaven* was one of his favorites: H-E-A-V-E-N— spelling and counting while imagining a rainbow. If another bad thing entered his mind, his panic soared and he'd have to start the ritual anew.

For three days he kept this up. Then he was told he was being removed from foster care and placed in the asylum in the country. With the crazy people and the perverts.

"I hope they shock your brains out. That's what they do there."

Bobbi Anne whispered she was sorry through his closed door the day before he left, and he whispered back that it was okay. She was scared because the shadow that hurt her would still be in the house after he left. There was nothing he could do to help her anymore.

After a few more parting swats in the kitchen he was able to get off the floor. He picked up the suitcase that his foster mother had thrown and got into the car.

Eight months with Bruce and Dorie and he'd hated every minute. He wasn't sure how he got there or why them in particular. It just happened.

"You can't stay here at your Nana's house no more." The lady who said this was from something called Social Services.

"How come?" He couldn't see why not. He had been always *here*.

"Why, child, Ruby . . . well, she's gone to heaven."

He looked back at Nana's cabin from his perch on the hood of the lady's Ford Fairlane. The car had two colors, white on the top and robin's egg blue on the sides. He liked how it looked. It was certainly better than Nana's old clunker, which was just brown and full of rust.

Inside the cabin, two deputies were talking loud enough that he could tell they were talking but not loud enough that he could make out the words. The door was partly opened, and he saw Nana lying on her cot near the stove. She hadn't moved the entire time the deputies had been inside. That surprised him. With guests in the house, she should've been up and about, chatting away and preparing something to eat.

The only sounds came from the deputies, who were standing out of sight because of the smell. At least that's what the deputies said.

He was confused. Though Nana hadn't gotten up from the cot for some days now, she'd asked him to prepare meals and wash up just like she always did. But now the deputies said she'd been dead for days.

For days. Good God, she was starting to rot.

He'd heard one of the deputies say this very thing.

He tried to explain that she'd talked to him this morning. But no dice. The preacher showed up after breakfast wondering if anything was wrong (he hadn't seen Nana in a while). The preacher was welcomed inside, and his eyes sprung open wide as one of Nana's dinner plates. The preacher called the sheriff and then all these people came over. Nana hadn't talked a single word since and it was now well after lunch.

"Where will I go?"

"We'll find a nice foster home for you."

He hated to leave Nana. She'd taught him other stuff besides preparing meals and washing up. Her cabin was in the country and well up the mountain. The nearest neighbor was a half mile away. There'd been plenty of coon hunting before their hound passed. She'd showed him how to snare rabbits. He'd skin, clean, and cook the animals. Then there was fishing. They went to the market in town, too, but the trip was long and Nana drove slower than molasses. She earned money mending clothes and sewing. People loved her crochet patterns.

There was always something new to see and understand.

He learned how to recognize wild plants and use them as medicine. She taught him which could be eaten and which were poisonous. He discovered how animals mated and made babies.

Most importantly, she taught him the rituals to keep the demons from coming out of their hiding places.

The gate had square brick pillars that reached higher than the roof of the car. Wrought-iron gates painted black were attached to the pillars by giant hinges. The tops of the gates contained row after row of sharp spikes that, in the hands of someone like a gladiator, could kill somebody easily. The gates probably squeaked when they swung open, but since they were already ajar he didn't know for sure.

The hour-long ride was completed in silence. The only words out of Bruce's mouth came while the news was on the car radio and he muttered something about that "fucking Kennedy."

That was fine with him. Bruce just bossed him around. *Hurry up. Get dressed. Clean this up. Help me do this.* Dorie was a little better. She baked cookies and let him watch TV sometimes. She got cranky, though, and would yell all the time when she was in a sour mood. Sometimes she'd spend days on end in the bedroom. Bruce wouldn't come home much when this happened. So it was up to him to take care of Bobbi Anne. Doing that was okay since Nana had already taught him what he needed to know.

Bobbi Anne was fun. He liked having a little sister. But she had nightmares, probably about the dark shape that hurt her. When he told Dorie what he saw, she screamed and cried. Bruce called him a liar. *Liar, liar, liar.* Bruce slapped him over and over. A couple of times he punched instead of slapping. Later that night he lay in bed hurting all over. Dorie and Bruce were hollering at each other, but then they quieted down. He heard Dorie climb the stairs to the attic, where his bed was, after looking in on Bobbi Anne. Dorie walked to his bed and lay down beside him. She said he was handsome. She smelled of liquor. He tried to forget what happened next.

The next day Dorie and Bruce called him wicked and dirty. He was the one who touched Bobbi Anne. (No, no!) He'd cast a spell on Dorie to make her do what she did. (What? No!)

Raised by a witch. What do you expect?

Bruce's '58 Olds 88 swung sharply into the driveway of Saint Edward's State Asylum. The car rolled, and he found himself sliding on his butt across the front seat toward Bruce. He grabbed the armrest to stop himself, but his leg touched Bruce right at the moment he stopped sliding.

"Get off me, you little bastard." Bruce shoved him back toward the passenger side while driving, swinging the wheel with his left hand.

"Sorry," he whispered.

Bruce seized a handful of his shirt while slowing the Olds in the circular drive near the front door. As the car halted, Bruce turned and pushed his face into his.

"Not one word. You hear me? Or I'll kill you. Don't think I won't."

Bruce released the shirt and smoothed out the wrinkles with the palm of his hand just as a lady in a brilliant white uniform approached the passenger side. Everything about her was crisp and spotless. She opened the door and stepped aside so he could step out. The lady was plump and not much taller than he was. Her big doughy arms wrapped around a clipboard held to her chest. Her white cap had a lot of folds and points, which meant she was a nurse. He expected her to be stern like his fourth-grade teacher, with glaring eyes and a frown. But she was smiling and her eyes twinkled. Strange, since she was about to lock him up in a mental ward.

"Oh dear." She rubbed a thumb on the dried blood on his cheek. "Looks like we had a nosebleed."

"Tripped over his luggage," Bruce said from behind the car as he unloaded the suitcase.

"My." The nurse flipped through some papers on the clipboard. "And you must be?"

"Cole Nightshade."

"Well. Welcome, Cole. We'll take care of you. We're one big happy family here."

Cole heard a hushed snicker behind the nurse. He searched for the source and didn't see anyone, mostly because his attention was drawn away by the scope of Saint Edwards. The building was huge. There were four floors with tall windows. The upper floor had all kinds of gables and spires.

Cole knew his demons were here and maybe other mean things. His heart started beating like a bass drum in a marching band. The sensation that something lurked just beyond his view—ready to claw or burst its way onto the scene—was overpowering. The pressure escalated, and only he could keep his world on an even keel. He focused on the trees in front of the building. As long as he counted an even number, he'd be fine. The tension would ease. There were eight. Phew.

With his heartbeat slowing, Cole glanced around. He was surprised at the number of people walking around outside. Big men with white shirts and white pants strolled slowly. They appeared to be keeping an eye on other people, all adults, who wore what looked like pajamas. The ones in pajamas were doing yardwork on the wide spread of lawn that surrounded the main building.

A throat-clearing sound came from the direction of the previous snicker. Cole could spot the source now that he had become attentive to his surroundings. An old colored man was raking a patch of lawn just a stone's throw away. He winked at Cole and pointed toward the sky. He silently mouthed something that Cole didn't understand. His suspicions about the setting started growing again.

Cole's heart leapt in his chest just like a startled rabbit. He counted windows to gain control and lost track at eleven. Odd number, not good.

"Now that's enough funny stuff, Lambert."

For a second, Cole thought the nurse might've been mad, but her lips smiled around her words and the old man chuckled. He resumed his raking until the nurse turned away and walked two steps toward Bruce, who by this time had dropped Cole's suitcase on the curb. Lambert gazed at Cole and raised his eyebrows. He pointed again to the sky and formed the words for Cole again. This time, he understood.

Watch out.

Frowning, Cole looked up. He should've started over counting windows, but his eyes followed the old man's finger. At first he saw nothing. Then he spotted an object launched from a window on the top floor, or maybe even the roof right above the main entrance where he was standing. It took a moment for the thing to come into view. It was a doll with something like a ribbon trailing in the breeze behind it. When the doll smacked the steps in front of the main door, it made a squishy noise and splattered all over. It didn't bounce like he'd expect a plastic toy to do. Then he saw why.

It was a baby.

Cole gasped, but he was the only one. No one else seemed to notice. The people in pajamas listlessly kept doing the yardwork. The men in white kept strolling. The nurse and Bruce were arguing.

"My wife filled out all them forms. I ain't coming in. He's yours."

"Mr. Asbury, you need to at least sign the admission form and let us inventory his belongings."

"I'll sign it right here. We don't give a shit about his clothes. He ain't coming back. The boy ain't right."

The nurse sighed and shuffled some of her papers to find the admissions form. She handed it to Bruce who, much to Cole's amazement, started reading it while leaning his hip against the Olds. Given how jumpy Bruce was acting, Cole had expected him to just sign the form and hightail it out of there.

The baby still oozed blood and sludge on the stairs. A howl pierced the air like a razor from somewhere above. Cole jerked his head upward to see someone diving from where the baby had been thrown moments before. This was a young woman or a teenage girl, he could see that clearly. The body descended in slow motion, twirling as it went. Cole thought she looked like a ballerina dancing on her way down. She was completely upside down when she hit the concrete. Her head smashed like a hardboiled egg. Her weight must've lent a little more force to both the arc of her fall and her landing than the baby's. She was farther down the steps at impact and rolled down the remaining steps.

Her body landed within a few feet of Cole. He scampered backwards and only stopped when his rump pressed against the car. Head swiveling in all directions, Cole didn't see a single soul who seemed to notice the gruesome wreckage in front of him.

The nurse was looking at him strangely. He kept waiting

for her to react, but she just turned back to Bruce, who was still going on and on about something. A breeze kicked up, and a flock of blackbirds landed on the lawn a safe distance away. Just like that Bruce and the nurse were finished.

"Get off the car, boy." Bruce practically broke his neck getting to the driver's-side door. His former foster father's hands fumbled with the handle like he'd never used one in his life. Fingernails clicked the metal under it.

Cole pushed himself off the car with his butt. He gazed at Bruce.

"Mind yourself." Bruce mouthed the words.

Cole glared and mouthed *Fuck you* in return. He'd never said it before, didn't know he had it in him, but it felt good. Bruce looked startled and stumbled into the car. He drove off without looking at Cole.

The whole thing was so strange that he nearly forgot about the splattered remains of the mother and baby in front of him. He swerved back to the mess, but it was gone.

Of course.

Still, he shuddered and counted his fingers on both hands while tapping his thumbs. Eight, still good.

A lanky teenage boy was staring at him from the top of the steps. His pants were a light blue, not like the all-white getup of the guards, or whatever they were called. That meant he was a patient. He wore a white T-shirt, though. And the sleeves were rolled up practically to his armpits. His hair seemed to be cut in the remnants of a flattop. His thumbs were hooked into his waistband. Cole thought he looked cool.

The teenager nodded at him.

Cole nodded back. The kid had been standing next to Lambert. Cole had a sense they'd been talking.

"Good, Kenny, you're here," the nurse said. She had appeared right next to Cole without him even knowing. She was a quiet walker. "You ready to come with me to show Cole around?"

"Yes, ma'am, I'll be delighted." He smiled a huge smile. One front tooth was positioned slightly behind the other.

"Wonderful." The nurse rotated and stepped in front of Cole. "We haven't been properly introduced. I'm Nurse Stern." She held her smile, but now it seemed faked. Her eyes were like a cloudy day. They didn't have any twinkles at the corners like people did when they were happy.

Cole stuck out his hand like he was taught. Nurse Stern ignored it. He let his hand slide down to his side.

"Time for you to be checked in. Pick up your suitcase and follow me. Kenny will inform you about life on the pediatric ward. Right, Kenny?" Nurse Stern looked over her shoulder.

"Yes, ma'am. I'll teach him all he needs to know." Kenny smiled again, and Cole's knees nearly buckled. Something about his words was scary.

As he followed the nurse and boy up the steps and past Lambert, the old colored man whispered, "You be watchful, Cole. Listen to Kenny and you'll be fine."

2
The Tour Begins

August, Present Day

THE EVENING TOUR WAS SHAPING up to be an impressive size for a Wednesday. A large party often made a difference, and today there appeared to be two large groups: a family of five, including three kids who looked between eight and twelve—ripe ages for ghost stories—and three middle-age couples who were clearly together based on their familiar banter with one another. Two especially hot college girls and an old dude who looked out of place made up the rest of the tour.

"Good evening, everyone," Chaz said to get the assembled group's attention. They had been chatting among themselves within their parties. The three couples were especially loud, and Chaz figured they'd had more than a few drinks during dinner at the Caretaker House. He wondered if the men would end up being pains in the ass during the tour, showing off for the wives or trying to be funny. Didn't matter. He could handle them.

"Welcome to Saint Edwards Mental Asylum. My name is Chaz Wimberly and I'll be your tour guide this evening."

One of the drunken husbands, a balding guy with glasses, turned to his wife, mouthed "Chaz?" and raised his eyebrows. She giggled behind her hand. Baldy was satisfied with her response and turned back to Chaz with a smirk.

Chaz blew it off. "Over here is Evie Blackstone. She'll be assisting me during the tour." He pointed in her direction, which was behind the group. Everyone turned to look and acknowledge her, but most had already been acquainted since she ran the desk in the lobby where customers paid the entrance fee. The two remaining shitfaced husbands, whom Chaz christened *The Beard* and *Potbelly*—for obvious reasons—exchanged glances and leered, although out of eyeshot from their wives.

Their reactions were understandable. Evie was mind-bogglingly gorgeous. Her hair was a flowing red that transformed into a burgundy shade in the right light. Chaz's heart palpitated madly every time he saw her. In fact, he'd fallen hopelessly in love with her the first time they met. As luck would have it, though, she wasn't interested in getting into a relationship. God knows he'd tried, and still did try in subtle ways. But he kept it cool. He didn't want to come off as some disturbed, stalking coworker.

He so much wanted to get her into bed. But they were just *friends*, she insisted. He had to satisfy his lust by taking things into his own hands, or more precisely his right hand, while fantasizing about how Evie might look naked. All conducted alone in his bedroom at home—his childhood home where he was still living with his parents, he was a little embarrassed to admit.

Evie had worked here longer than he had, two months

longer to be exact. She'd taught him everything she knew about Saint Edwards, so they rotated the tour-leader duties. And they both pitched in with staffing the gift shop, cleaning up after the tour, and preparing for the next one. They also worked on revising their scripts, deleting and embellishing as needed based on patron reactions.

"The tour should take about an hour or maybe a little more, depending on what we see or...experience."

Smiles from the family of five. Good. This pause before "experience" often produced smiles or nervous chuckles. The hot college girls, both heartbreakingly blond, leaned into one another and squealed. The trio of couples nodded. Not bad.

Only the old dude remained impassive. Maybe he was one of those scientifically minded types who took the fun out of the tour for the whole group. His dress pants, button-down shirt, and tie—although the knot had been pulled away from his neck and his top button was open—only added to the party-pooper image. Chaz would need to work on him.

"However, we'll gladly give you enough time for questions and pictures. And yes, please take time for pictures. You never know what you might capture in a photo that couldn't be seen with the naked eye. Afterward, we also keep the gift shop open for your perusal of our official Saint Edwards selections." Chaz smiled as best he could. He disliked the sales pitch because it felt beneath him, but he was amazed at how many people did stop and buy T-shirts, coffee mugs, postcards, and other shit.

As planned, Evie strode through the group to join Chaz. "How many of you are guests of the inn located on our campus?" Another marketing ploy.

The three couples raised hands, with two or three adding,

"We are." The old dude briefly pointed an index finger upward.

"Wow, excellent," Evie chimed, pumping her fists at the same time.

She was so good at this. Even the word "campus" added a certain charm to the entire setting. It also lent a certain level of seriousness to the entire enterprise.

"The grounds are quite big, really," Evie said. "In addition to the asylum, which is huge in and of itself, there are green areas that the patients used for exercise and the caretaker's house, which was masterfully transformed into the inn."

The latter wasn't entirely true. There had been some kind of structure behind the asylum, probably a barn or storage shed. All that had remained of it after the facility was shut down was a pile of wood and portions of a foundation. An impressive and historical-looking mansion was built on the spot for the sole purpose of being an inn. The final structure was christened the Caretaker's House when it opened for business.

"The owner, Ambrose Rutledge, purchased the entire campus and buildings five years ago to save it from demolition. He had a relative who'd been a patient here many years ago and felt it important to preserve the property and tell its story. While the history is fascinating, not all of it is positive. Terrible things happened here. And the consequences of those awful things have lived on and remained in this asylum today."

Evie's comments were more or less true. Rutledge, whom Chaz had met once six months ago, was a filthy-rich dude nearing fifty who was on his second or third trophy wife. He had more money than he knew what to do with, so he bought the asylum, which had been sitting vacant for God knows how long. In addition to some ancestor of his residing here, Rutledge also had an interest in the paranormal and saw this place as a hobby, if not a goldmine.

That suited Chaz fine. Saint Edwards was right up his alley too, for many of the same reasons. Chaz was enamored with ghosts and the paranormal, and this work was giving him great practical experience.

Chaz took over the opening remarks. "Mr. Rutledge isn't done with the grounds. He has plans for this asylum over the next few years. He wants to renovate parts to their original glory." He paused for a reaction. Sometimes this remark fell dead. Other times folks smiled at the improbable juxtaposition of "original glory" and old mental asylum. There were smiles now, even from the old guy. His smile had an edge of cynicism to it, though. Something about the angle of his head telegraphed the old guy's scorn.

"Other areas have yet to be renovated. You may see some worn and deteriorated places from a distance. Graffiti on the walls. That kind of stuff." Chaz looked to the family. "Offensive words have been covered or removed." Mom nodded gratefully. The kids' expressions fell in disappointment.

"Most areas of the asylum are safe. They've been examined by our own engineers and those from the state. So rest assured. Anyway, in a few years' time, Mr. Rutledge plans to have the lobby and a couple of the wards in pristine shape, and they'll be available for rent for weddings and proms. You name it."

That always brought a laugh regardless of who spoke it.

"Listen, I'd love to have my wedding reception here," Chaz added, as he often did for the groups. He wasn't sure if this comment made him attractive or creepy to Evie, but she never rolled her eyes, which he counted as a plus.

3

Slaver and Stern and the Demons

KENNY WASN'T SCARY AT ALL once Cole spent a little time with him. He wasn't mean like some bigger kids could be and was way nicer than Nurse Stern. She made him feel uncomfortable because everything about her seemed faked. Kenny was different. He seemed trustworthy.

Nurse Stern led Cole and Kenny through the main door toward a reception desk.

"I've got young Master Cole with me. I'll check him in upstairs. Can you contact Dr. Slaver?" Nurse Stern's iced smile remained intact for the receptionist, who had a pencil behind an ear. Her blue-tinted gray hair covered her ear in such a way that Cole at first thought the pencil was sticking out of her head. His heart flipped in his chest.

"Yes, Nurse. Right away." Her voice was no-nonsense as she reached for a phone.

Kenny placed a hand on Cole's shoulder and gently pushed. "Upstairs, now, Nurse?"

"Yes, young man. Let's keep things moving."

At these words, Kenny whisked Cole down the hall and under a huge arch that was almost long enough to be a tunnel. The wood inside the arch was comprised of panels, and Cole knew from his time with Bruce that paneled walls were a sign of good craftsmanship. Even more impressive was the curved paneled ceiling underneath.

Emerging from the arch, Kenny maneuvered Cole to the right without a word. They headed to a broad staircase that went over the hall they'd just come through. It really was like a tunnel.

"We'll fill you in later," Kenny whispered. "But here's a couple of things. For now, just say yes or no when they ask a question. And always 'sir' and 'ma'am.' Got it?"

"Yes, sir."

"Not to me, man." Kenny snorted and sharply turned his head to check on Nurse Stern. Cole did the same and found her multiple steps behind. She was looking at his file as she walked, not paying attention to them.

"You're going to get a physical from Dr. Slaver, even though he's a headshrinker." Kenny leaned closer to Cole and whispered more softly. "He's gonna ask you if you masturbate. Just say no. They think kids who do it are homosexual and they give you shocks to your head if they catch you."

Cole swallowed. "What?" He wasn't sure what that even was.

"Not so fast, Kenny. Wait for me," said Nurse Stern as they started up the grand staircase over the arch. With the slightest tug on Cole's shoulder, Kenny stopped their progress.

"Yes, ma'am."

Kenny turned briefly to Cole. "Later," he mouthed.

Nurse Stern passed them and led the way upstairs. She turned left toward a closed door at the end of a short hallway. A bundle of keys appeared out of her uniform like magic and she unlocked the door. She stepped aside to let them enter.

Cole found himself in a large room with cream-colored tiles from the floor to halfway up the wall. The rest of the wall was painted a light green that reminded him of the gunk that he blew out of his nose when he had a cold.

"This here's the common room. We can talk, play games, and sometimes watch TV if the picture comes in good." Kenny spread his arm as if the room was his very own creation.

There were three girls and one boy in the room. The boy was rocking back and forth in his seat and looking at a *Life* magazine spread out on a card table in front of him. One girl was curled up in a chair snoozing. She was ghastly thin. Skeleton girl, Cole thought. Another girl was the exact opposite. She pranced counterclockwise around the room, and the fat on her hips jostled with each step. She made grunting noises that might have been an attempt at singing. Cole saw right away that she was mentally retarded. He could tell by the shape of her face.

The third girl was listening to rock 'n' roll on a transistor radio. Cole liked listening to the radio. The girl must've noticed him because she looked up.

"Kenny, who's that?" her voice boomed.

"His name's Cole." Kenny used an announcer's voice for the benefit of the entire room.

"Hey, Cole. You like music?"

Cole nodded, not knowing if he was allowed to talk. The girl had breasts under her T-shirt, so she was older than him, maybe fourteen or fifteen. She also had angry red marks carved into her face in crisscross patterns. Somehow that made her look prettier than she already was.

"Shush, you two. No need to yell," Nurse Stern said from behind them. "Cynthia, you can talk to Cole later after we check him in."

Cynthia tsked loudly and thrust her head back with an exaggerated groan. Cole thought it was funny but tried not to smile.

"Don't get overexcited, dear." Nurse Stern's lips tightened into an icy grin. Cole bet that she didn't like being disrespected, but she was letting Cynthia's response slide for now.

From his left, Cole heard a rolling sound. He turned and saw a glass enclosure with two nurses behind it. One of them was a man who was sliding open a glass window on a counter. He leaned out and said, "Excuse me, Nurse Stern, the doctor will see our new admit in twenty minutes. Want me to clear out the shower?"

"Thank you, Dale. Yes, that would be wonderful."

Cole's eyes shifted to Kenny. The other boy shrugged. "Part of check-in. You shower, get new clothes, see the doctor. Usually not this quick, though. You're lucky."

"We'll talk later. You can listen to the radio too." Cynthia was standing right next to him. Cole hadn't heard her move closer. He felt panicky for a second, like he couldn't breathe. She was taller than he was, although not as tall as Kenny. They were like giant trees blocking the sunlight. He counted Cynthia's eyes and then Kenny's. Four, a safe even number.

"Okay, Cole. Come with me," said Nurse Stern.

Cole recalled Kenny's advice. "Yes, ma'am." He nodded to Cynthia, who surprised him with a wide smile and a wink.

Nurse Stern passed Cole as she walked down the hall past

the nurses' station and away from the common room. Her white nurse shoes squeaked on the floor which each foot lift.

"Kenny, stay close. You're not done yet," she said without turning her head.

Behind Cole, Kenny groaned softly. Nurse Stern stopped in her tracks and twirled rapidly. Her smile glistened like the polished blade of a sword.

"I'm sorry, dear. What did you say?"

Cole watched Kenny. His expression slackened and he stood stock still. "Nothing, ma'am. I'm glad to help."

"Delightful. That's what I thought." She spun on her heel and resumed walking.

Cole wondered what the heck had just happened.

The shower sequence was embarrassing. The man nurse, Dale, was standing outside the men's room.

"All clear."

"Very good. Now, if you could get Cole's belongings— just those that he'll need, of course."

"Will do." Dale handed some items to Nurse Stern and left his post. He strolled down the hall. One of the kids in the common room said something Cole couldn't hear, and Dale replied that he'd be back soon. Cole looked back at the nurse.

"After you, Cole. Kenny, you too." Cole entered and sensed Kenny right at his back. The bathroom had urinals, stalls, and two sinks on his right. To his left was a doorway without a door. Inside he saw five shower stalls. There were shower curtain rods for each one, but no shower curtains.

"Take off your clothes and give them to Kenny."

Cole was stunned. He couldn't move.

"Young man, you don't have anything I haven't seen before. Now hurry. The doctor's waiting."

Kenny looked at the wall as if something interesting was up there. Cole turned his back and undressed. He clumped his clothes into a ball and passed them behind him to Kenny without turning. Kenny must've still not been looking.

"Kenny."

His clothes were lifted from his hands.

"Bend over, Cole."

What?

"Bend over and spread your cheeks."

Cole had never done this before, but he had an idea what she meant. He blushed as he did it. He couldn't imagine why she'd be looking up his butt. Fortunately, it was over in a moment.

A hand appeared over his shoulder as he stood up.

"Here, this is shampoo."

Cole took a tiny paper cup that had some yellow liquid in it. Another hand appeared. "And you can use this soap." The soap was really only a sliver. Cole doubted he'd get much lather.

"Now go. You have five minutes."

Cole scampered into the little shower room. He was relieved to see she didn't follow him in. He took a stall that was out of Nurse Stern's line of sight. The shower was similar to the one in his foster parents' house, so he knew how to work it. The hot water wasn't very hot; he barely needed to budge the cold water faucet. The water initially stung the cuts on his face, but the pain was over before he could react. After that, the soft stream of warm water was soothing. He imagined the dried crust of blood melting from his face.

"Three minutes left."

Cole turned to see if she was watching, but she was still out of sight. He decided to hurry then. The shampoo was like baby shampoo, and he rubbed the soap over his body until it disappeared.

"Almost done?"

"Yes." Then he remembered. "Ma'am," he added. "I'm rinsing off."

"Here's your towel." Nurse Stern's voice carried well over the water. She was still in the next room.

Cole turned the faucets off and felt chilled. Without any sign of movement, Kenny had appeared in the doorway. He was facing Cole, staring over his shoulder.

"Here." He held out a folded towel.

"Thanks." Cole rubbed his face and moved to his chest. Kenny turned so his back was to Cole and leaned against the doorframe. He started talking like he was reciting something in school.

"We wake up at seven thirty, get dressed, and go to the dining area for breakfast. The dining area is right by the common room. You didn't see it before."

Cole took the towel in both hands, pulled it back and forth behind his back, then shifted down to his butt. He listened closely.

"This is the boys' wing. We have our sleeping area; it's like a big room at the end of the hall. And it's round. We have a little table next to our beds and a little locker for our underwear and socks. We can't wear our clothes from home. They store them away somewhere. We gotta wear these hospital-issue clothes. They're like pajamas. Normally we wear slippers, but we can use our sneakers if we play outside or in the gym."

"How come we can't wear our sneakers all the time?"

"Because they don't want anybody killing themselves."

Cole frowned. "How can you kill yourself with sneakers?"

"The shoelaces. You can hang yourself."

Cole finished drying and wrapped the towel around his waist. He never would've considered that. "Oh."

"The girls live on the wing on the other side of the common room. The common room and the nurses' station are in the middle. You can't go down the girls' hallway without permission, and they can't come down our hallway."

Nurse Stern shuffled papers around the corner. The doorway to the bathroom swung open.

"Why thank you, Dale."

"You're welcome. Anything else right now?" Dale's voice floated into the shower room.

"That's it." Cole heard the door open and swiftly close again.

Kenny turned to Cole. "Your clothes are here."

Nurse Stern's hands came into view and handed Kenny the clothes. The older boy grimaced slightly, but his face quickly returned to a passive expression. He held the clothes in front of him. Cole dressed, thankful that the nurse wasn't watching him.

♑

His pants were a light blue and, as Kenny had said, felt like pajamas. They fit okay. The T-shirt was a little big, but he rolled the sleeves up like Kenny did with his. His socks and slippers were given to him in the hallway where it was dry.

A man who looked like he'd just sucked on a lemon came down the hallway pushing a big cart that said Laundry. His shirt had the word *Maintenance* written in script above his left pocket on his chest.

"That's Daniel," Kenny said as the man came closer. Daniel scowled at Kenny, then grinned.

"So, a new boy," Daniel announced to the hallway. He

turned his attention to Cole. Nurse Stern pursed her lips in disapproval.

Cole didn't know if he was supposed to answer, but he took a chance. "Yes, sir."

"Gettin' the tour, huh? Talk to me sometime, I'll show you things around here that'll curl your hair."

Kenny beamed at the remark, but Nurse Stern glared at the man. "That's enough, Daniel. There will be none of that."

"Ha. Which? Curling his hair or showing him the skeletons in the closet?" The maintenance guy said this like either option would be fun to do.

Cole was astounded that someone would defy Nurse Stern. She wasn't pleased either, continuing to scowl at Daniel.

"Well, anyway, Cole. We'll see you around. You can just throw that towel in this here cart and I'll take it from you."

The damp towel was still over his shoulder. Cole grabbed it and tossed it in. "Thank you."

"Don't mention it. Enjoy your first day." He glanced toward the nurse. "Nurse Stern." He bowed and moved on.

Nurse Stern straightened her already steel-like posture. She took a slow breath and exhaled. Her tight smile returned to her face.

"You were quick in the shower, Cole, thank you. Now let's go upstairs to see Dr. Slaver. Kenny, you can continue with your talk."

The physical part of his exam with the doctor was uncomfortable. Nurse Stern came in the office with him while Kenny sat in a wooden chair in the hallway outside the door. Cole stood next to the doctor's desk after being guided there by the nurse's forceful hand.

Dr. Slaver didn't look up from his desk right away. Cole saw his name on the sheet of paper before the doctor. There were other words on the page, too: *belligerent, angry, obsessive-compulsive rituals, sexual experimentation.* Cole swallowed involuntarily. Some of those words he understood. Others he didn't.

Dr. Slaver raised his head. His eyes were bulging like they were going to pop out of his head any second. They were green like moss from the forest where he lived with Nana. His lips were puffy and colorless except for a section by the lower corner where the skin had been picked off. Tiny scabs and a flaky pink covered that area. He looked like a fish that had just had a hook removed.

The doctor rotated in his chair. He placed his hands on Cole's shoulders and patted them, then did the same to his hips.

"Hmm. Sturdy boy." This he said over Cole's shoulder to Nurse Stern.

"Yes, Doctor."

"There's an exam table over there," he said to Cole, looking back down at his notes and pointing. Cole turned to his right and noticed for the first time the table that had a partition with a white curtain at its head. The table looked like it had green leather skin.

"Take off your shirt and pants and sit."

Cole obeyed and wondered if the doctor would give him privacy by moving the partition. The doctor rolled over to the table—the chair was on wheels. The partition stayed where it was.

The doctor moved the stethoscope over his chest and back while telling him to take deep breaths. A little hammer tapped right below his knee, and his lower leg jumped up. Cole couldn't help grinning. The doctor didn't notice or care. At one point, Cole observed that he had hair growing out of his ears. It was almost as thick as the hair thinning on top of his head.

"Stand up."

Cole hopped down, and before he knew it, Dr. Slaver had pulled his underpants down. They settled around his ankles. He gasped when the doctor grabbed his balls. Nurse Stern had shifted her position to look directly at his private parts.

"Do you masturbate?"

Say no.

Still he couldn't speak. The doctor's hand seemed to squeeze again.

"Well?"

"No." Cole could only manage a squeak.

The doctor nodded as if he was satisfied. Only then did he remove his hand.

"You can get dressed."

Cole didn't waste a second. He put his clothes on in a blink of an eye.

"So, do you see these demons?"

Cole sat in a hard-backed wooden chair on the other side of the desk from the doctor. Nurse Stern sat to the side, facing Cole. Her chair had padding on the seat and back.

"No, not really. I kinda *feel* them."

"Now, Cole. What does that mean? You feel them." Nurse Sterns smile was plastic. The doctor looked at her and frowned at the interruption.

"Just that. I get the sense they're there. Like a movement in the corner of my eye."

Cole remembered back to a few years ago when his Nana talked to him about this. He was feeling jumpy and worried

about being alone. He hated leaving her when he rode to
school on the bus every day.

"You're feeling nervous a lot more aren't you?" Nana
asked.

"Yes'm." He looked at the wooden planks below his feet
that made the small covered porch outside the back door. It
was spring and getting warm. Birds were chirping and insects
were coming alive in abundance.

"What happens when you feel like this?"

Cole knew he could trust Nana with the truth. She'd
never laugh or tease him. "My mind sees terrible things. Like
you dying or the cabin being washed away in a flood. Sometimes I'm alone and all these arms are trying to yank me away
and bring me down into the darkness."

"Oh, my. That would be scary."

"And I feel this burning, sick feeling in my tummy and it
spreads all over."

Nana frowned a tiny bit and nodded. "We all have our
own personal demons, Cole. Those are yours."

"Really?" Cole had never considered this.

"You can do things, you know, to keep them from trou-
bling you."

"I can?"

"Oh yes, child. You have the ability. You'll be able keep
them under control and they'll never be able to touch you."

Cole looked at her and waited for more. After a few
moments, Nana surprised him by asking what kind of pretty
pictures he could look at in his mind. Well, that was easy.
He had some happy images of her that he especially liked.
Her walking in the forest teaching him about the animals,
her baking pies and giving him a taste—all the while smiling
or laughing out loud. There were serious mind pictures, too.

Her collecting herbs or concentrating on the approaching weather.

"So, what do you think? Can you erase the scary pictures and put these happy pictures in their place?"

Cole pondered this. "I guess so. But I bet it would get tiring to do these things."

"Oh, yes, it can. I know."

"You do?"

"This runs in the family."

They talked some more and came up with other ways to distract his mind when he felt the demons trying to make an appearance. They concocted strategies with numbers and letters, and Cole tested them out. A few days later, he came to Nana explaining the strategy he'd decided upon.

"When I have to do it, I count things. Or think of words and count the letters. Even numbers are good. Odd numbers, not so good, so I have to keep going until I count something that ends on an even number."

This, more or less, is what he stuck with. The problem was that he had to work extra hard a lot of times to defeat the demons, usually over and over again, and the whole thing was tiring—just like he'd suspected it would be. And he often worried about whether he was doing it perfectly and what would happen if he messed up.

"Young man?"

Cole had been a million miles away. The doctor's stare was piercing, and he had one eyebrow raised practically halfway up his forehead. Nurse Stern patted her pad with the eraser of her pencil.

"Um, sorry. I was just...thinking."

"Thinking? Whatever about, dear?" Nurse Stern asked.

"My nana. She taught me how to keep the demons away."

"The ones you just feel and don't see?" The doctor's eyebrow was back in its normal location. His glare remained.

"Yes, sir."

The doctor leaned back in his chair, which creaked and squealed in response. He tapped his chin with an index finger. Cole counted the taps and there were four. The finger remained stationary on the doctor's chin. After a few heartbeats, a fifth tap was added. Cole's anxiety jumped.

"You saw the demon once, though. A shadow that went after your foster sister." Dr. Slaver's lips turned up at the ends. Cole had the feeling the doctor was trying to trick him.

"I thought so at first," Cole said. He paused, not knowing whether to go further. He decided to chance it. "Then I realized it was Bruce who hurt her."

Nurse Stern sighed loudly. The doctor's eyes shifted in her direction and returned an instant later to look back at Cole. The nurse's interruptions bothered the doctor.

"They said it was you who hurt the girl."

"No. No, sir. I wouldn't do that." Cole tried to sound earnest but it came out like a whine.

Nurse Stern jotted something on her pad.

"What did your nana teach you to do to keep the demons at bay?" The doctor leaned forward again, and he seemed genuinely interested.

Cole described the counting process and how he sometimes added pleasant pictures of things to help out—especially if the word for the pleasant thing had an even number of letters.

"But sometimes the counting does the trick?"

"Yes, sir. Like before. You tapped your chin five times and I got worried."

Dr. Slaver acknowledged this observation with a "hmm"

and sat up a little straighter. Even Nurse Stern was watching him closely.

"But I'm not feeling any of them right now, so it wasn't too bad. If there was one, I would've needed to find something else to count to bring it up to an even number."

"That's fascinating." If anything, the doctor's eyes were wider than before. Cole imagined them flying out of his head with loud pops. It wouldn't take much to make them leap.

"I tell you what, Cole. We're going to do some observing of you over the next week or so. No medication for you at this time."

That sounded like a good thing. The frown on Nurse Stern's face looked like it was set in stone, though. Not a single muscle moved. Maybe she didn't agree with the doctor.

After the unsettling visit with Dr. Slaver, Cole received the continuation of the typical-day-at-Saint Edward's tour from Kenny. Meals were prepared in a kitchen in the rear of the building in the basement. Patients considered trustworthy and safe, like Kenny and Lambert, retrieved the meals and transported them on carts to the appropriate units of the asylum. Lambert took his portions to the two men's units—one of which was for violent patients who were kept segregated from everyone else. Kenny brought his to the women's unit and then the kids' unit. Kenny liked going to the women's unit, which was right above them on the third floor. The patients there were a mixed bag; some were really crazy and didn't do much but sit or stand around. Others doted on him like a mom. Occasionally, there would be younger women who'd say dirty things that turned him on. One time a woman was able to get her hand down the front of his pants and touch him before the nurse stopped her. He looked for her every time he went, but he never saw her again.

Showers were in the evening before bed.

"That's when you can play with yourself safely."

"What?" Cole said.

"That's why I told you to answer the doc's question no. They think you're a faggot if you masturbate. They try to cure you with electric shock. But they give you some privacy in the shower, so yank away there."

Dale was all right as far as the staff went. He played ball each day with the boys when they went outside, weather permitting. He also overlooked minor transgressions. And he allowed them to talk with other patients, assuming it was safe. This was how the kids had gotten to know Lambert. The old man was as safe as could be.

After dinner was pretty boring. You talked, read, or watched television if the reception was decent. Bedtime was early, ten at the latest. But no one complained because it would eventually get back to Nurse Stern, who'd end up giving everybody a lecture in group. Group time varied, but it happened almost every day and could be excruciating. Lectures on behavior and feelings, Kenny said, often proved tiresome or embarrassing.

Kenny's tour ended a little before dinner. All in all, he made Saint Edwards seem almost normal and not like the awful place Bruce talked about.

4

Things Get Creepy

September 1962

"You lucky dog. No medication," Cynthia said.

They sat at a circular table for four people. Dinner was almost over, and Cole had finished eating all the food on his plate twenty minutes ago. Cynthia gave some of her "chopped steak" to him after she had a few bites and declared it gross. She gave some to Kenny, too, since he'd finished his plate about a minute after Cole. They had carrots as the vegetable, sliced thinly so they were kind of mushy. Nana's had always been always crisp and flavorful, not like the tasteless clumps he'd just eaten. Still, he was starving after his first day and practically inhaled everything.

The skeleton girl and the prancing girl sat at another table. The skeleton girl didn't touch anything on her plate except a slice of carrot. The prancing girl ate all of her food but didn't use utensils. Her immediate surroundings were a mess.

Cole *was* relieved about not taking any medicine. "Yeah,

I guess I'm lucky. I didn't know they could give you pills here. I thought it was just shocks."

"Who told you that?" Kenny asked.

"My foster father."

"Sounds like an asshole."

Cole considered that. The crude word fit perfectly. "He was. For sure."

Cynthia and Kenny nodded although they hadn't ever met Bruce. They just seemed to understand.

There was someone else sitting at their table too. Timmy was a strange kid. He usually didn't look at anybody and sometimes repeated what people said. He could answer questions if you asked, but his voice sounded weird. It reminded Cole of Robby the Robot from that movie *Forbidden Planet*—one of his favorites. Right now, Timmy wasn't talking much, but he appeared to be concentrating on what the others were saying.

"You both take pills?"

Kenny shook his head and rolled his eyes. Cynthia was a step behind him in replying, "Yeah, Thorazine. I take more than Kenny does."

"Why?"

Timmy rocked in his seat. "Because his behavior is under control."

"Damn, Timmy. You sound like Nurse Stern," Cynthia said.

"Damn, Timmy. You sound like Nurse Stern," Timmy said

Cynthia groaned but smiled shortly thereafter.

Timmy continued his recitation. "Cynthia's mood swings are more severe. Kenny's anger is way down." He rocked some more.

Kenny laughed. "God, Timmy. Now you're like Dr. Slaver."

Kenny was the leader of this small group. He was the oldest and had been here the longest. Cynthia and Timmy were both the same age, fourteen.

Because Kenny was doing well in the asylum, he had gained some status. Nurse Stern was grooming him as some kind of an assistant.

"If this was a prison, they'd call me a trustee," Kenny had said earlier when they carried their plates back to the table. "Anyway, that's why I was showing you around today. I'm being trained to help out. It's supposed to be an honor, I guess." Kenny shrugged.

Cynthia leaned forward and whispered. "He knows how to play the game. You're good at it." This last line was directed at Kenny.

"Damn straight I am."

Cole was impressed. "So, you get what, extra rewards or something?

"Privileges." Kenny pointed his plastic fork at Cole. "Extra privileges and responsibilities. I can go all over the place without supervision. Well, almost all over. Usually when I have these small jobs to do. I can bring you along if I'm with a staff person."

Cole thought that might be interesting. Since his return from the doctor's office, he hadn't felt anxious or worried about his demons. Somehow being with these kids kept him distracted. Cole marveled at the experience.

The dining section of the ward, along with a small kitchen area, was off the common room. Every room that Cole had been in had large windows, but they were covered with something to keep people from escaping. Their sleeping area had bars, the common room and the dining area had heavy-duty screens. The bars and the screens were attached to black metal frames. A staff member could insert a key into the frames surrounding the bars or screens and they'd swing inward on hinges. This would allow access to the windows so they could open or close them. On this particular day, the windows were open so the ward could enjoy the early-evening refreshing breezes. The day had been hot for September, and the building's interior would be sweltering if the windows were closed.

With dinner completed, Dale gave the signal for after-dinner chores. A couple of kids swept the floor, others wiped down the tables. Cole was assigned to wash and dry the dishes with Cynthia.

"We use this stuff so no one tries to kill themselves," Cynthia explained as they worked on crappy plastic dishes, cups, and utensils.

"I never knew there were so many ways you could do it," Cole said, somewhat awed.

"Yeah, well, I guess people have tried." She sponged the crud off the dishes and rinsed them.

Cole retrieved the clean items from a drying rack and dried them with a dish towel. He stacked the dishes on the closest table in the dining room. He placed the dried cups and plasticware next to the dishes. Midway through his job, the towel was too wet to get the job done. Dale showed him where to hang it and get a new one.

When Cole was drying his last cup and Cynthia was wiping out the sink, Kenny—who had table-wiping duty—slipped into the kitchen to rinse out his dishrag. He glanced around to make sure that Dale was still distracted in conversation with another patient.

"Cole saw the leaper this afternoon."

Cynthia gasped. "No. Really?"

Cole looked from one to the other. "What?" he whispered. No one else had reacted to the girl and the baby splattering on the steps in front of the building, which made him think he was the only one to see it, except that odd old man named Lambert. While Cole knew how to distance himself from awful memories, Kenny being aware of what happened really knocked him off-balance.

"Hold on, how'd you know?"

"Easy, man," Kenny said. "Lambert told me. He's a seer. He says you're one, too."

A seer?

Cynthia's jaw dropped. Cole could've fit an orange in her mouth, it was so wide.

"Oh my God," she said after she got over the initial shock. "You can see the spirits who haunt this place." At her side, Kenny nodded briskly.

"Kenny, let them finish their chores. Out of there," Dale called from the opposite side of the dining room.

"Yes, sir. Sorry."

"Grab those corner seats," Cynthia whispered fiercely as Kenny backed away from the kitchen. She jerked her head toward the common room. "We need to talk about this."

Twenty minutes later, Cole and Cynthia sat on a couch in the common room. Kenny sat on the floor in front of them, leaning against the wall with his long legs stretched out before him, cotton pants rolled up to over his knees because of the heat. The couch had been a gold-and-rust-colored plaid at one point but was worn to nearly threadbare condition after years of hard use by teenagers and kids. An oval, braided rug that was a mixture of greens and blues sat in the center of the room. A couple of easy chairs were scattered around. Nothing matched, and nobody seemed to care. A television with lousy reception was mounted on the ceiling. A game show was on; no one paid attention to it.

Timmy sat nearby in an uncomfortable-looking plastic chair, looking at a book about planets and rocking slightly. Cole had a feeling he was listening in on their conversation.

"So you saw them all smashed up and everything," Cynthia said.

Cole nodded.

"Blood running and everything." Cynthia needed to double-check everything.

"Yeah. I said that."

Cynthia seemed to process this information. Above and behind Kenny's head, a window provided a view of the Blue Ridge Mountains, which weren't blue at the moment but cast in a deep green shadow. The sun was setting behind the highest peaks, its golden light becoming diffuse and transforming into a hint of violet. The shadows enveloping the mountains would soon take over the entire landscape.

The transistor radio played softly. When they first sat down, Cynthia wanted to appear like they were having a normal conversation so as to not arouse suspicion. Kenny said that Dale was okay and wouldn't give them too hard a time for talking among themselves as long as they didn't look like they were conspiring to do something.

"So, Lambert said he's a seer." Cynthia directed this statement directly to Kenny, who nodded. "Okay, now. That's good. Now we have our own seer instead of just Lambert. You can tell us about the ghosts."

"That's what a seer is? Someone who sees ghosts?"

"That, and other things," Kenny said.

"Like what? Don't just stop there."

"Well, you should know. Don't you just sorta know things? Know what people are thinking and stuff?"

Well, that was true. Nana had been dead for a couple of days before the preacher showed up, but they'd talked each of those days. And hadn't he gotten the sense that Bruce was going to do something with Bobbi Anne? And that's why he was spying on her bedroom door?

Kenny continued his recitation. "Lambert says that some seers can, you know, influence other people to do stuff or move objects just by thinking about them."

"Huh. I can't do that."

A scream jolted the room. Cole nearly jumped out of his skin, and Cynthia swore out loud. Timmy yelled, "Shut up" in the direction of the screamer, which surprised Cole since he'd been pretty low-key since they met. Kenny was the only one who didn't react. He kept looking at Cole and seemed cool as a cucumber. He didn't even flinch.

The scream came from the heavy girl, who had given up her prancing for coloring with crayons after dinner. Something had gone wrong with her drawing. She threw a crayon and bellowed another piercing scream.

"Uh-oh. Another tantrum," Cynthia said.

Dale entered the common room from the nursing station. "Easy, Beatrice. Calm down."

Beatrice didn't. She screamed again and kicked the table. Another nurse appeared out of nowhere carrying a hypodermic needle, followed by two men in those white uniforms that Cole saw patrolling the grounds when he arrived. The four of them wrestled Beatrice into a headlock while the second nurse gave her the shot. Within seconds, the screams dissipated into sobs and the crowd of adults escorted Beatrice down the hallway in the direction of the girls' rooms. The sobs ended before the sound of keys jingled.

Cole's mouth hung open. He felt his heart racing in his chest.

The wall under the television wasn't flat and solid anymore. It heaved and rippled. The shape of a face formed under the plaster as if it was made of rubber. Below that, hands pushed outward from the wall.

A demon was going to force its way from behind the wall. Cole was going to actually see one instead of just feel it.

"What's the matter?" Cynthia's head appeared in his line of sight. She looked into his eyes, then looked at the wall and back to him. "What do you see?"

Cole started counting magazines on the table before them.

1-2-3-4-5.

Damn. There had to be another. There on the floor. That made six.

1-2-3-4-5-6.

He tapped his index finger into his opposite palm with each number. The face and hands withdrew slowly as if the wall was deflating.

Cole exhaled. He hadn't realized he was holding his breath.

Cynthia stared with both hands covering her scarred cheeks. Her eyes were wide like bottlecaps. After a few seconds, the corners of her mouth curled in a tiny smile.

Kenny remained stretched out on the floor, but he looked—and there was no other way to describe it—like he was impressed with Cole.

Dale was looking at him, too, from the hallway. He

must've just returned from the girl's hallway. His expression suggested he was more concerned.

Cole cleared his throat and tried to look nonchalant. Dale's gaze lasted only a second more as he filed back to the nurses' station.

"You look like you just saw a ghost," Kenny said. He brought his legs under him and stood up in one motion. He sat down by Cole's other side. "Okay, spill."

Cole didn't want to look at the kids on either side of him. He dropped his eyes to the floor. "Not a ghost. A demon."

Cole had spent the last couple of years trying not to think of the demons. But here he was for the second time that day describing all their nitty-gritty details and the rituals he went through to ward them off.

"So, you've never actually seen them?" Cynthia said.

By the end of his recitation, Cole had scooted back so far that he felt like he was sinking into the couch. Both Cynthia and Kenny sat cross-legged, watching him. Even Timmy had turned his chair around to face Cole. His planet book was upside down on his lap, clearly forgotten.

"They weren't demons."

This came from Timmy. Cole and the others turned their heads in unison. Cole was about to ask how he knew that— after all, it was *Cole* who saw them—when Timmy resumed. "It's simple. Cole's a seer and he saw the leaper. He never saw his demons before. Therefore, what he saw was some kind of ghost. Not a demon. It's obvious." Timmy sat back in his chair and picked up the book from his lap.

Everyone remained quiet until Kenny cleared his throat.

"I think he's right. It makes sense."

"But—"

"No buts. The rules don't change like that, do they? No. Next time, don't count or anything. Let's see what happens."

"Easy for you to say."

Cynthia shifted and moved one leg so that her foot rested on the floor. The scarring on her face, the cruel straight lines on her cheeks and forehead, seemed to cast their own thinly drawn shadows. Cole wondered yet again how she got them.

"Something you need to ask Lambert about when you get a chance. I wondered if it could've been the Creeper." Cynthia turned to Kenny. "But, he doesn't show up like that, does he?"

"Nope. He comes in the dark. And from the dark."

"Who's the Creeper?" Cole asked.

"He's been haunting this place forever. If you see him, you're dead," Kenny said.

"And he eats children," Timmy said.

"He saves their skin, too. And wears it around on top of his skin," Cynthia added.

Cole blinked. "You're lying."

"Swear to God, no," said Cynthia. "That's the truth. Ask Dale, even. Any adult will tell you."

"Have you seen him?"

Kenny snorted. "No, man. If you see him, you're *dead*."

Cole stretched out on his back in bed. The night was muggy, so he kicked off the top sheet. The windows had no curtains, so a nearly full moon cast a pleasant silvery light across the large room. Three of the five beds were occupied. Timmy was on the other side of the fan pattern while Kenny was in the bed next to Cole's. Like Cole, Kenny slept on top of the sheets. His lanky figure was almost too long for the bed. Based on their breathing, Cole could tell the two older boys were asleep.

Cole folded his hands atop his chest. He sensed rather than felt his heartbeat under his ribs.

The day had been strange.

What began as a series of frightening and humiliating incidents ended, well, a lot different than he expected. He couldn't say he was happy or he'd had fun. But he met these new kids and he liked them and they seemed to like him. Who could've predicted that on his first day in an asylum?

Cole sat up in bed. He looked toward the dormitory door. It was shut, but a window in the middle showed the hallway leading to the common room. Off to the side, Cole could see the edge of the nurses' station. Beyond the common room was the hallway to the girls' rooms. He wondered why the girls had individual rooms and the boys had to share one large room. Sharing didn't bother him, though. In fact he kind of liked it. There was safety in numbers, and he was glad Kenny and Timmy were right nearby.

Cole dropped softly back to the bed. Outside a breeze picked up and pushed the humidity lazily around the dorm. His skin felt damp. If he could see his face in a mirror, it would probably look a little flushed.

Sounds of animals paraded across the asylum grounds. Cole was used to them. After all, he had lived with Nana in a mountain cabin, and animals were frequently in the vicinity. Here it seemed different, though. The crowd of wildlife seemed more expansive. Chirps, cheeps, squeaks, growls, and moans volleyed from one end of the grounds to the other. He even imagined various cries coming from deep in the mountains. The sounds seemed more agitated. He couldn't explain why. They just did.

Cole recalled a time when he was walking in the early morning. It was summer and hot like now. He might've been nine when this happened. The heat made it difficult to sleep, so he got up and dressed. When Nana wasn't inside the cabin, he went for a walk to find her. Cole strolled up an easy mountain path Nana used frequently. The shade was plentiful, which made it one of her favorites. She also found many of the plants used for herbs and medicine along this way, too. It was a good bet that he'd run into her sooner or later.

Mountain laurel bushes drooped a little from the heat, but not so bad that a thunderstorm wouldn't perk them right up. At a small ridge, Cole looked for Nana but didn't see her right off the bat. He wasn't concerned; he knew the area like the back of his hand, and Nana was around somewhere. He turned back to try a different route and stopped abruptly.

Standing five yards away was a girl he'd never seen before. She was scrutinizing him, and Cole almost laughed at her expression. She had hair the same deep black as his. Her eyes were dark blue like he'd see at dusk on a cold winter day. He found her quite pretty. The girl smiled at his reaction, and Cole guessed she was an older teenager.

"Hi," Cole said. His voice sounded crisp despite the muggy air.

The girl didn't reply with words, just her smile, which widened a bit more. She took a step up the path. Cole noticed that she was wearing a skirt, which was a weird thing to have on in the mountains. He took a few steps down, almost close enough to touch her. She mouthed the words *I love you* and raised a hand to her face. Tears sprang to her eyes but they were happy tears—she was still smiling.

"Violet."

The word was spoken in the tiniest of whispers behind Cole. He whirled around. Nana was there on top of the ridge. She held a basket in her hand that contained wild herbs and berries. Nana had the same kind of smile as the girl. And the same kind of tears.

"Nana," Cole said with his own smile. He returned his attention to the girl.

She was gone.

Cole gaped and swiveled his head from side to side.

"Did you see that girl?" His heart was leaping with the wonder of it all. He wasn't scared, just confused.

Nana was quiet as she climbed down the mountain. She watched her footing over the rocks and roots in the path. When she reached Cole, she placed her arm around his shoulder.

"Well, did you?" The suspense was getting to him.

"Let's go have some breakfast, shall we?"

They began walking. The bushes and wildflowers leaning into the path brushed his bare legs and arms like feathers.

"Nana, c'mon. Who was that?"

She stared ahead as if looking at the distant mountain peaks. "We'll talk at home. I promise."

In the kitchen, she made biscuits. While those were cooking, she made compote with the berries picked that very morning. Cole knew well enough that he couldn't hurry her when she was in the kitchen. He'd have to bide his time while she baked which, when you were nine, was the hardest thing.

When she finally sat down with him at the table and said grace, Nana looked like she was ready to talk. She waited, though, until he sliced open a biscuit and slathered it with warm syrupy fruit.

"That young lady had hair just like yours. Did you see that?"

"Uh-huh," Cole said around a mouthful. He swallowed. "Jet black. Like mine."

"And her eyes?"

"Yep. Very blue."

"So blue, they're almost violet," Nana said. "And again, they're just like yours."

"Like mine?" Cole had to think about this.

"Yes, the same shade of violet. When she was born, I saw those eyes and I knew what I would call her. Violet." Nana smiled a sad smile.

Now Cole was puzzled. He had only a tiny bite of biscuit left, and he could easily have popped it in his mouth. Instead, he dropped it on his plate. "But..."

Nana leaned over and took his face in her hands. Her smile remained and so did her tears. "She was my little girl. And she was your momma."

Now that it was out, Cole had to admit that it wasn't a complete surprise. The hair color gave some of it away. The eyes even more. And really, the words *I love you* kind of fit. It was like the last jigsaw piece falling into place.

"She's dead, right? That's what you've always said."

"Sadly, yes. When you were just a baby. So many things got the better of her. I've told you that your worries run in the family. Well..."

The last piece of biscuit made it to his mouth. Cole chewed and considered this.

"So, she's a ghost?" Cole didn't know what to make of that.

"A spirit, maybe. I don't see her often. It must've been your time. One of the gifts you have is a certain sensitivity to these experiences, my dear child. I've noticed that in you."

At the time, Cole didn't quite follow what she meant.

Now, lying in bed in an asylum, he understood.

I'm a seer.

※

A noise like a swinging door invaded the quiet of the moonlit dormitory.

Cole sprung up to a sitting position and grabbed his ankles.

"What?" Kenny was alert in his bed. Cole would've thought he was still asleep.

"Shh."

Cole swung his legs over the bed till his feet landed on the floor, paused momentarily, and then stood.

The door to the boys' dormitory was propped open. It had been closed before, Cole could've sworn. He scanned the room and saw nothing out of place. Timmy was motionless in bed. The sheets on Kenny's bed were rustling and the mattress springs wheezed. Kenny was getting up.

Cole pierced the indirect light in the common room down the hallway. A lone figure stood in the shadows. Rags and remnants of old clothes draped the figure's shoulders. Cole squinted and gasped. The head was misshapen and hideous. A mask of unnatural horror flashed by in an instant as the figure dashed for the door of the unit and crashed down the stairs.

"What happened?" Kenny stepped beyond Cole. His body blended with the shadows in the room, although his white jockey shorts reflected the silver moonlight.

Cole rushed after him and clasped a hand on his forearm. "Wait. I saw something."

"What?" Kenny's voice was impatient.

"A monster," Cole said. "The Creeper."

"Nah. That's bullshit. He woulda killed you for sure. C'mon."

Kenny strode toward the hallway to the common room. He slowed at the propped-open door long enough to whisper over his shoulder. "Normally they keep this closed." He continued past the bathroom and to the common room.

Cole was at Kenny's heels, trying to keep up. A step before they entered the room, the screaming began. Cole flinched and clasped his hands over his ears.

"Now what?" Kenny hissed.

"God almighty. Don't you hear it?"

Kenny looked at him. Clearly he didn't. "Hear what?"

Cole entered the room and took his hands from his ears. His eardrums felt like they were being impaled by screwdrivers. The screams came from all directions. The lights of the common room were off, so his ability to see came only from the moonlight shining through the windows. Even the nursing station was dark.

"Who turned off the lights?" Kenny asked from his side.

Cole could only shake his head. His attention was focused on the walls, and it was all he could do keep from wetting himself.

Faces and hands. Ten, twenty, thirty sets—Cole couldn't begin to count—pushed desperately against the wall, stretching them to nearly the bursting point. Impressions of open mouths were distinctly visible in the skin of the walls. The surfaces vibrated with the release of every anguished cry.

Cole swung to face Kenny. "The walls are screaming." He feared his head would burst with the sound.

The overhead lights came on. The impact was almost physical as Cole and Kenny recoiled with the illumination. The screaming in Cole's ears snapped off in the same instant.

"What are you two doing out of bed? You shouldn't even be in here." Dale stood at the entrance to the unit. He was holding a soda can in his hand. "I'm gone one moment to the vending machine and you try and break out. In your skivvies, no less."

"We thought we heard something," Kenny said.

"So you thought you'd investigate."

"Well, yeah."

Dale smirked. "Just get back to your dorm and get to bed." He motioned for the two of them to get moving down the hall. Cole led the way, assuming Kenny would follow.

"Wait," Dale called.

They turned around just past the bathroom.

"Who opened the door?" He pointed.

"It was like that," Cole said.

"That's how we heard the noise out here," Kenny lied.

"That door was closed." Dale walked past them and examined the door. There was nothing visible propping it open. He pushed it with his fingertips, enough to initiate a slight change in position. It moved forward until it gently shut and tapped the doorframe with a tiny click.

Dale looked at Cole, then Kenny. "You guys didn't do this?"

Both shook their heads.

"Well, that's weird." He opened the door again and let it go. The door shut on its own.

"Okay, enough strangeness for one night. In bed and don't get up till morning."

Cole and Kenny walked side by side to their beds, not saying a word. The only sounds were Timmy's gentle breathing and cries of wildlife outside their windows. Silently counting each of his steps and tapping his fingers for extra emphasis, Cole was relieved that the count was twenty-two when he reached his bed and plopped down.

5

Warming Up the Crowd

August, Present Day

"A LITTLE KNOWN FACT," CHAZ announced once the group assembled on the third floor. "For a short time, the asylum served as a sanatorium for tuberculosis patients. This was in the late nineteen teens to the early nineteen twenties."

Evie had informed Chaz that starting on the third floor and working down to the basement was the way to go for the most thrills. You could start off edgy and get downright creepy by the tour's end using that strategy. Chaz had a different view—the basement was kind of a letdown—but he went with her approach. At least the group would spend most of the tour going down instead of up. They typically herded the group up to the third floor, where the history of the place was summarized. The fourth floor was off-limits because there were still piles of crap up there that needed to be cleaned and, more importantly, there was nothing but dated, boring offices to be seen.

"That little fact may come up again when we make

our way to the basement area. Before serving as a sanatorium, however, the place was initially built as a private boy's school."

"A boy's school?" A squeak from the middle kid in the family, a boy of around ten.

"That's right, a boy's school. A boarding school, really."

"Wow. What ages?" From one of the wives in the trio.

Evie chimed in to make the experience feel more interactive. "High school."

"A football powerhouse for a short time, weren't they?" the old dude asked.

Chaz was impressed, and he could tell Evie was too. "Yeah. Not many people know the history."

The old dude shrugged as if it wasn't a big deal.

"The headmaster recruited strong athletic kids for that very purpose. He felt athletic prowess was more important than academics. The school won state titles and even played UVA and Tech a couple of times. Won, too." Chaz wasn't sure of this last detail, but who was going to check?

"What happened to the school?" Potbelly asked.

"Evidently, it wasn't financially sound. Educating a bunch of jocks, let alone trying to feed them, was expensive even back in the day. Then there was an issue of hiring and keeping staff. Plus, there were rumors of money embezzlement." Chaz shrugged.

"When did it close?" From the dad.

"The best we can figure, early nineteen twenties. Maybe mid-twenties. The sanatorium was opened shortly thereafter. When that closed..."

Evie was on her mark. "Saint Edwards Asylum was born."

"Our first stop is the door on my right." Chaz pointed, and everyone turned. "The Women's Ward."

"Ooooh," said the Beard. His wife thought he was a riot. She snickered and playfully slapped his upper arm.

The youngest kid pressed against her father, who ruffled her hair. She put on a brave face and smiled up at him.

Evie made a big show out of unlocking the door to the women's ward—in reality the lock was a simple deadbolt—complete with the haunting thud of the bolt sliding open. She led the group into the ward, moving far enough forward so there were no stragglers in the hall. Chaz brought up the rear and let go of the door, allowing its hydraulics to move it slowly back into position. It shut with a subdued yet decisive click.

Pure atmosphere.

Evie began her talking points. Chaz would contribute some theatrics in a few minutes.

"You'll find the floor plan of each unit to be similar. The center is comprised of a common room and a dining room. Off the dining room is a small kitchen. Meals weren't prepared here. Instead, they came from the large industrial-sized kitchen in the basement. Well, depending on how you identify your floors, the kitchen could be the basement or the ground floor. Since this asylum was built in a mountainous region, the terrain dips quite a bit across the expanse of the foundation. What might be basement for some parts of the hospital was ground floor for the kitchen. This also permitted direct access for deliveries and such."

Evie stepped further into the space of the ward. She extended both arms and pointed in opposite directions. "There are two hallways. These were the patients' bedrooms."

The mom raised her hand.

"Yes?" Evie said. Her grin welcomed all questions.

"This looks quite nice here..."

One of the sloshed assholes snickered.

Mom didn't care. "So, this has been renovated. Is this the plan for the whole hospital?"

"Eventually, yes. This area has been cleaned, painted, and restored to its original décor. As best as we can determine, anyway."

"Restored to the original décor of the asylum for sure," Chaz said. "The records for the school and sanatorium are lost."

Mom nodded in response. Evie continued, "In addition, parts of the pediatric ward and some of the treatment rooms downstairs have also been done. The men's wards, there were two, are now underway. They need the most work. We won't be able to visit them. Some individual rooms and hallways still have a lot of decay and graffiti."

The twelve-year-old waved timidly. Evie motioned to him.

"How come there were two for the men?"

Evie clasped her hands with glee. "I was wondering whether anyone would catch that." The kid loved her reaction. He grinned bashfully.

God, she was good at this.

"Yes, there were two wards. One of them specifically reserved for violent patients. The other was for the nonviolent ones. Those wards extended out behind the building. The violent ward had its own exercise area, surrounded by fencing and topped with barbed wire. Each ward had a separate entrance and exit. The one for the violent guys was accessed from outside or from the basement. There weren't actually many on that ward, though. Most men who committed violent acts would just go to prison."

"Why are the men's wards taking longer to renovate?" This from Baldy.

Evie's smile diminished in intensity to suggest the seriousness of the impending revelation. "There was some serious
structural damage that had never been adequately addressed.
A tornado hit the asylum back in the early sixties and did
considerable damage. Some patients lost their lives." Additional atmospherics.

Time for Chaz to jump in and provide the first spooky
accounts of ghost sightings.

6

Worst Birthday Ever

September 1962

Cole woke with a start and sprang up.

For a panicky second, he couldn't recall where he was. Then, seeing the five beds in a fan-shaped pattern along the curved wall, the memory came crashing back. The asylum.

He collapsed back in bed.

"Now, young Master Nightshade," Nurse Stern called from the doorway. "No more sleepyhead. Up now, along with the rest of you."

Nurse Stern strode into the room with her chin raised. Cole wondered if she smelled something bad or was just trying to look like she was better than everyone else. Her doughy arms clasped her clipboard to her fluffy chest. Behind her was another nurse, who was younger. She had dark hair that didn't seem real. It was all loops and curls and waves. How her cap remained in place was a mystery. She didn't smile like Nurse Stern's fake smile. In fact, she didn't smile at all. Her mouth was a straight line and her eyes were the color of mud puddles. She looked like she was trying to be tough. There were pimples on her forehead, though, and that kind of ruined the effect.

"Stand at your bed, boys."

Cole was first up. Nurse Stern gave him a plastic smile. Kenny only groaned and buried his face in his pillow.

"Kenny, now." The tone wasn't angry, but there was authority behind it. Kenny moaned again and lifted himself from the bed. Timmy was already standing and wiping sleep from his eyes.

"Now, Peggy, let's check the sheets."

The young nurse took four quick steps—Cole counted them—and placed her hands on his bottom sheet. She smoothed it with her palms and stood up. With a nod to Nurse Stern, she proceeded to Kenny's bed and did the same. The young nurse's attention flickered a brief moment when her eyes skirted Kenny's face. Then it was gone, replaced by her previously serious expression. Whatever she saw regarding Kenny's sheets satisfied her, and she signaled as such to Nurse Stern.

A longer string of steps brought her to Timmy's bed. She leaned in, appeared to sniff, and ran her hands across the sheet. She stopped abruptly, bending farther to get a closer look at something. She stood after a short time and directed her attention to Nurse Stern.

Cole watched the routine with amazement. He couldn't imagine what was going on. Next to him, he thought he heard Kenny swear under his breath. He glanced at Kenny. The older boy just shook his head.

Nurse Stern placed her right hand on the middle section of the lower sheet. She traced something circular and tsk-tsked while rising.

"Now, Timmy," she said. Her voice sounded like she was disappointed. Timmy just looked around the room. He didn't seem especially troubled.

"Timmy," Nurse Stern said again. "There is a boy stain on this sheet. You know what we talked about."

Timmy started rocking on his bare feet.

"Did you hear me?"

"Yes, ma'am."

"Well, we'll need to watch this or have another session with the doctor."

"No, no. Please, I won't do it anymore. It was an accident." Timmy's eyes widened.

"Well, that's neither here nor there. We'll watch and make sure. This is certainly not normal and needs to be corrected. Soon." Nurse Stern's voice took on an irritated tone. Timmy shouldn't be arguing with her.

"All right, now. All of you make your beds and go into the bathroom to wash up for breakfast. Then come back to get dressed."

Breakfast was simple. Choices of cold cereal with milk and orange juice. The morning and noon meals were carried in by trusted patients from the women's unit. They were gone in a flash, but not before they marveled over Cole.

"Ooh, you're new," gushed a motherly type. "What's your name, sweetie?

Cole didn't know if he should say anything. He stammered for a second before Cynthia came to his rescue.

"That's Cole."

"Cole. I like that name. You'll need to come visit us." The motherly type beamed. Next to her another older lady nodded with a big grin. Her head bounced so fast that Cole worried she might hurt herself.

Cole finally got his verbal bearings. "I will if I can." What else could he say?

"Maybe a dinner run, Kenny?"

"That's what I thought I'd do, Mrs. D," Kenny said as he reached for the box of Frosted Flakes.

All the while, Nurse Stern stood in the background listening. Her face didn't give any indication as to how she felt about Cole visiting other wards.

The three boys and Cynthia sat together again. Beatrice and the skeleton girl sat at another table with the nurse named Peggy. Cole needed to learn the skeleton girl's name soon.

When Nurse Stern was out of earshot, Kenny leaned over his cereal bowl. "Timmy, I told you to do it only in the showers. It leaves stains when you get it on the sheets."

Timmy looked around without meeting anyone's eyes. There was the tiniest lift of a shoulder which could've been a shrug.

"What are you talking about?" Cynthia's gaze bounced back and forth between Kenny and Timmy.

Kenny quickly summarized the morning's sheet check. Cole was surprised at how comfortable he was with talking about such a thing.

"Timmy." Cynthia used a scolding voice. "You know how you hated the shocks the last time."

Demons seemed to be pressing in all around Cole just out of his vision. His anxiety heightened. "They gave Timmy shocks for...touching himself?" Cole counted each side of a door while tracing a rectangular shape on his thumb using his index finger. It was an easy *1-2-3-4* even-number count. When he still imagined the demons approaching, he added the diagonal lines, which brought it up to a pleasing count of six. As was often the case, this needed to be repeated to gain a sense of control.

"Yep, it's unnatural, Nurse Stern said. And a sign you're a homo." Kenny glanced around to check for any prying. "That's bullshit. Dale said so. But Slaver and Stern think it's true."

Cynthia leaned in and faced Cole. "They're supposed to put you to sleep and relax your muscles so you don't get hurt during the shock. But for this, they don't. They think you need to feel it in order to make you stop."

Thoughts of shocks and demons were putting Cole on edge. The idea of one alligator-clip jumper cable attached to his dick and the other to a car battery made him squirm. This image was followed by the sensation of invisible forces pressing both sides of his head. Cole pictured his skull being squished and exploding as if it were a volcano with his brains pouring out like lava.

He needed to walk around and focus on his counting. Sitting at the table just wasn't going to cut it.

"I gotta go to the bathroom." He scrambled away, counting as he moved down the hall.

After about a minute, maybe less, Cole started calming down. The worst symptom was lightheadedness, which he eased by throwing water on his face and swishing his mouth. He leaned on the sink and stared in the mirror. Without warning, he felt like crying. His chest welled, but he forced the feeling down with an intense will. He'd be damned if he stated weeping now.

"You okay?" Kenny entered the bathroom. Cole hadn't heard the door open.

"Yeah." His voice quivered the tiniest bit. "I started feeling weird."

"Well, Stern is pissed that you ran off without asking. She sent me to get you."

Cole rolled his eyes. "I'm supposed to ask?"

"Yeah. We'll probably cover this in group."

Kenny led him out of the bathroom. Cole paused after a step.

"What's group again?"

"You're about to find out."

The eating area had undergone a transformation since he went to the bathroom. The tables had been pushed as far as they could go toward the back wall. The chairs had been arranged in a circle close to the windows.

Nurse Stern and Peggy were already seated. Nurse Stern looked snooty, her posture all angles and stiff as hardwood. The white skirt of her uniform was tucked neatly and tightly under the backs of her thighs. Cole expected her to yell at him for his improper departure. She only nodded once in his direction, but her look could've set kindling on fire. The young nurse, Peggy, also glared at him, although she wasn't as good at it. There was no believable threat behind her expression. The pimples on her forehead made her look like she was just another kid. She crossed her arms tightly over her chest as if she was cold—or leery of her role.

There were only two chairs available for sitting, one between Timmy and Cynthia and the other between the skeleton girl and Beatrice. Kenny and Cole hesitated as they approached the group. Kenny signaled for Cole to take the seat by Timmy and Cynthia. Grateful, Cole took a step in that direction.

"No, Kenny, you sit by Timmy," Nurse Stern said. "Cole, sit between Beatrice and Laura Jean. Thank you."

Cole exhaled and slunk over to the empty chair. Beatrice made a whinny sound and clutched her belly. The skeleton girl didn't move a muscle. She had brought her knees up to her chest, and the heels of her slippers rested on the edge of her seat. Cole couldn't imagine how she could fit in that position on the chair.

At least he'd learned her name. Laura Jean.

Over his right shoulder the windows were open and humid air furled into the room like a rolled-up wet towel. Humidity muffled the sounds of patients outside working on the grounds or walking. More obvious was the chattering of birds. Cole turned and saw some sparrows flapping each other on a concrete slab serving as a sill outside the screen. A crow landed and scattered the sparrows, who complained as they took off. More black crows moved in and squawked as they faced the window opening. Their calls increased in volume to a panicked screech. Cole counted six of them—an even number, but still, he felt like they were yelling at him.

"Go away." Peggy appeared at the screen and hit it with the back of her hand. "Scat. You're making too much noise."

Cole's heart beat rapidly. He hadn't even noticed her moving to the window.

"I never seen them do that before," Peggy said as she strode back to her seat.

"Nasty things, really," Nurse Stern said. "Rats with wings."

Nana would've agreed. There was something about a lot of crows that meant something bad.

After Peggy returned to her chair, Nurse Stern began.

"Well, good morning to you all. We have some important items to talk about." Nurse Stern's fake smile was on full display. Cole peeked around the circle. Nobody was looking at her. They were staring at their hands, their knees, or the floor.

"Does anyone have something they'd like to share?"

Faces remained averted until Timmy waved his hand.

"Yes, Timmy?"

"Cole has purple eyes."

Cole hadn't anticipated this. Naturally, all the kids looked right at his face. So did Peggy and Nurse Stern. Beatrice stood and pressed her face within inches of Cole's. Her breath smelled rank. She grunted something unintelligible which could've been "purple" and sat down.

Cole felt bashful and would've turned his face toward his lap if he hadn't caught a glimpse of Cynthia's expression.

"Timmy's right," she said with a wide smile. "Although I think they're more like violet."

Cole appreciated her words.

"My, they do have a certain hue you could call violet. They're like the blueish purple at twilight. Very unusual." Nurse Stern maintained her porcelain smile.

"Twilight eyes," Timmy added, and smiled to himself.

The group shifted back to an awkward silence. After a few moments, Nurse Stern filled the void.

"I'd like to start with a happy piece of information." The smile was even wider, but with no light behind it. "What's today's date?"

Nobody moved. Cole saw Kenny shift slightly out of the corner of his eye. Peggy stared right at him. Her pimples were a painful-looking pink against her pale skin.

"Oh, come on now. We keep track of the dates. The calendar is on the wall in the common room."

Cole hadn't noticed this.

"Kenny. Surely you must know."

Kenny was staring at his right pants leg, which was crossed over his left. "September tenth."

Nurse Stern beamed. "That's right. Now, what's special about September tenth?" she gazed directly into the face of each kid. Then she looked at Cole. "Cole, what's special about today?"

Cole sat there not able to move. He had no idea. He could only stare back at her. Just as he broke eye contact and averted his gaze to the floor, it hit him. It was like getting clobbered in his face with a pillow during a pillow fight. His lips curled slightly and he looked back at Nurse Stern.

"You forgot, didn't you?" Still the frozen fake smile. "Happy birthday, Cole."

Crap, it was his birthday. And he was spending it locked up here.

Still, Cynthia and Kenny were gawking at him with wide grins—and they were genuine.

"How old are you?" Kenny asked.

"Twelve." Cole felt a little embarrassed for some reason.

"Well, happy birthday," Cynthia said.

"Yeah, that's neat. Happy birthday," Kenny said. Timmy was rocking in his seat, but he winked at Cole. Beatrice and the skeleton girl didn't say anything.

Nurse Stern wiggled a little in her chair as if proud of herself. "Now, let's talk about our next item of business."

Despite the initial pleasantries, an air of wariness settled on the room. Cole felt a blackness, a pressure, on both sides of his face. He turned slightly to his right and left. There was nothing to see beyond the windows and the tiles covering the lower part of the wall. He had the feeling of demons, however, so he counted the squares on the floor. Within their immediate circle there were eighteen full ones, so that worked out. His tension eased slightly.

"Cole?"

"Yes, ma'am?"

"Are you listening?" Nurse Stern stared at him, no longer smiling. Beside him, Beatrice grunted.

"Yes, ma'am."

"Good, maybe you can tell us what 'respect' means?"

Cole's eyes darted around the circle. The nurses stared at him, and he felt like a bull's-eye. Kenny also looked at him, but his expression was unreadable. Cynthia was biting her lower lip and she seemed worried. Could this be a trick question like at school? He didn't know.

"Um...it's like treating people the right way." Cole hoped that was right. He sort of remembered the word from school.

"Yes, I think you can say that. When you treat someone in a dignified manner you're being respectful."

A breeze picked up outside. The leaves on the trees were rattling more than they had earlier. The sky was hazier, too. Nana had taught him that when this happened, it meant it might rain in a few hours.

"Have we all been respectful of others here in the ward?" The extra-wide smile was back.

The other kids were focusing on anything but Nurse Stern. Cole kept an eye on her because he couldn't tell if she wanted him to answer. She wasn't looking at him, so he hoped he was off the hook.

"Beatrice, do you remember last night?"

Beatrice mumbled and groaned. Cole couldn't tell if she was answering or even understanding the question.

"You screamed and carried on, dear, while you were coloring. And you threw a crayon."

The breeze kissed the side of Cole's forehead with muggy air right through the screen. Otherwise there was no sense of movement in the group. Even Timmy's rocking stopped. For her part, Beatrice clenched herself into a statue.

"Were you respectful to the other children in the ward when you screamed? Hmm? Beatrice?"

The girl's head started vibrating as if she wanted to shake her head but her muscles were stuck.

Nurse Stern lost her smile and her face was firm. "Was your carrying on respectful of other people's comfort and feelings? The men who had to hold you down and escort you to your room? The other children? Was that respectful?"

There was no way Beatrice could understand these questions. Cole felt stricken by the interrogation and he wasn't the one under the spotlight. Then, to his complete surprise, Beatrice's head started shaking *no*. The movement continued and became more rapid with each pivot. She made *eek-eek* sounds in her throat for emphasis. Although she stopped after a few seconds, the exchange was so painful to watch it felt like hours.

"Very good, Beatrice. So we can expect better behavior on your part tonight, right?"

Beatrice moved her head up and down. So, she did understand.

"Now, let's talk about bedtime rules. Kenny?"

Kenny's head picked up. Peggy watched Kenny intently as if something important was going to happen.

"Yes, ma'am?"

"Bedtime rules. Why do we have them?"

Kenny's eyes looked far away. "We need the rules so that we can have restful sleep. Sleep is healthy for growing bodies and minds. And we can't disrupt other patients' sleep." The reply was automatic. Cynthia grinned but quickly made her expression blank again.

"So, walking around after lights-out in the common room wasn't a good idea was it?"

So that was where this was going. Cole felt bad since he was the one who got up first, but Kenny was getting the lecture.

"No."

"No, what, dear?"

"No, ma'am."

"No, it wasn't. Do you think that was respectful of the rules? Respectful of others who might've had their sleep interrupted?"

Kenny stared back at Nurse Stern and didn't reply right away. When it looked like she was going to say something, Kenny snuck in a "No, ma'am."

"Were you respectful of the new patient? Leading him to break the rules on his first day?"

Cole was ashamed. He opened his mouth to say "It was my fault," but Kenny rushed his reply this time.

"No, ma'am. It was disrespectful to mislead Cole, I'm sorry." Kenny glanced at Cole as he said this and shook his head once.

"Very nice, Kenny. I'm proud of you," Nurse Stern said.

Cole thought she actually did look proud. It was like Kenny was her star patient. Peggy's expression said the same.

"Now, what about self-respect? Timmy? Have you been respecting yourself?"

Timmy resumed his rocking. His back was slapping the back of the chair pretty hard. Cole thought Nurse Stern would find this annoying, but she acted like she didn't see it.

"Self-respect also means not violating nature. Did you know that, Timmy?"

No response from Timmy. Peggy looked disgusted.

Still, Nurse Stern's voice was gentle even though the words would've cut the average kid mercilessly. Cole didn't understand what she was talking about at first. When it dawned on him, he lowered his head into his hand and covered his eyes.

"When you spill your seed, you're violating nature. In so many ways. That's true for all boys." The latter remark was intended for Kenny and him. Cole could tell by the increase in volume as she rotated to take in the circle.

"So, we will be keeping watch, Timmy. Do you understand?" Her tone was like January ice.

"Yes, Nurse Stern." The rhythm of the rocking slowed.

Nurse Stern didn't keep Timmy on the ropes like she did with other kids. Cole wondered if she thought Timmy was a lost cause and had given up hope. And if so, what it meant for Timmy.

A gale forced wind swooshed through the windows. Hair was blown every which way, and a few loose napkins on one of the tables went airborne like kites and sashayed to the floor.

"Oh my," Nurse Stern said with a chuckle.

Birds shrieked on the concrete sill. Cole turned and saw that the crows were back. There were too many to count, and his heart jumped into his throat. Their caws were like nails on a chalkboard.

Nurse Stern rearranged some papers on her clipboard. Peggy, who'd been bothered by the crows before, didn't react to the interruption. The other kids didn't seem to notice either.

Pounding noises began right above them on the next floor. The sound reminded Cole of soldiers in training who were running in army boots—at least in terms of the loudness. The precision was missing, as the pounding noises appeared to ricochet off each other in a random pattern of drumbeats. What was going on?

The two nurses sat impassively as if waiting for somebody to say something. Cole looked to Kenny and found him staring into space. Cynthia looked bored. How could they miss this noise?

Somewhere on their floor, doors started slamming. Cole couldn't help but count them. He wasn't sure how many there were initially, but once he started, he counted to ten and stopped there. The slamming continued. There was no way there were that many doors on their ward. They had to be continuously opening and closing on their own.

Nurse Stern looked at him, her head tilted like she was watching him with one eye through a microscope. Peggy leaned forward and watched him curiously.

The shrieks from the crows outside the window were replaced by a human scream.

Cole turned in time to see a nurse falling in slow motion from a floor above his. She landed headfirst on the concrete slab outside the window, and then the rest of her body slapped the ledge. Her uniform ripped open and her body split like sausage casing. Her guts splashed the screen. Blood shot through the tiny holes to cover Cole's face and arms.

Oh God!

He shot to his feet and opened his mouth to scream, but nothing came out. The body of the nurse, whose uniform was stained with splashes of red and gray, leaned toward the edge, paused for a moment, and fell out of sight toward the ground below.

Cole looked at the closest person to him, Laura Jean. The skeleton girl returned his gaze, looking shocked. She unfolded herself from her fetal position on the chair. The skin on her arms was pulled taut over her bones, which were sickeningly detailed. Patches of skin were so delicate they looked transparent. Veins stood out like bluish-green ropes.

Laura Jean raised her head to look at him. She had the face of a cadaver. Her eyes floated in tissue-thin skin within their sockets. Her mouth opened, and Cole was certain her jaw made the noise of a screen door that needed oil.

Cole fell to his knees.

"Cole? Cole?"

Cole gasped.

Kenny was on one side of him and Peggy on the other, holding him up as he knelt on the floor.

God. What was that?

He scanned the room. No guts on the windowsill or the screens. He checked his arms. They were clean. No slamming doors.

"What the hell happened to you?" Laura Jean said while facing him from her seat. She still was thin like a skeleton, but no longer a corpse.

Cole couldn't bring himself to look at Nurse Stern. He looked at Kenny instead. His friend stared back with a neutral expression. After a few heartbeats, Kenny whispered, "You okay?"

Cole could only nod. He knew he was in trouble. He lifted his head and faced Nurse Stern.

She was not concerned. If anything, she looked . . . interested.

"Well, Cole. We're glad you're back. How are you feeling now?"

He said the first word that came to his mind. "Stupid."

"Oh, dear, there's nothing to feel stupid about. We're here to help you."

~~~

Cole would've loved to disappear into a corner somewhere. He felt like the whole world was watching him and whispering things. Kenny pursed his lips together, nodded, and gave him a thumbs-up. At least he was impressed. Timmy's eyes were like hubcaps for minutes afterwards. Cynthia looked worried and took to sitting as close to him as possible. Cole thought she wanted to ask him what happened, but Nurse Stern dragged him to the nurses' station immediately after group. Her grip on his upper arm was like the jaws of a lion.

Nurse Stern started pumping him for an explanation as soon as she sat him in a chair. Peggy came into the glass enclosure to listen. She was standing right behind him.

Was he seeing his demons?

Well, no, he didn't think he was.

What then?

He didn't know but had a feeling it was ghosts.

Ghosts?

Yeah, ghosts. The ones that haunt the asylum.

What ghosts? What did they do?

Cole didn't want to tell her everything. He mentioned how out of the corner of his eye he thought he'd seen someone falling from a floor above. That sounded safer. After all, people saw things in their peripheral vision all the time. Maybe she could appreciate how alarming it might be.

No such luck. She kept probing him for additional hallucinations—which is what she called the experiences. He didn't want to report on the leaper lady and her baby from yesterday. That seemed, well, too much. Reluctantly, he spilled the beans on the slamming doors, the harassing birds, and the horrifying transformation of the skeleton girl. He even provided a little more detail on the falling nurse. Her pressing continued. *Was that all? Did you see anything else? Are you sure?*

Cole didn't report anything else. Still, Nurse Stern didn't seem satisfied. After moments of quiet that felt like hours, she dismissed him. As he walked out of the station, Cole saw her reach for a phone. He observed her as long as he could as she talked animatedly with someone. Then he was out of view of the glass partitions.

Cole took a seat in the common room. Cynthia and Kenny made a beeline for him.

"Man, what'd you see?"

The breeze swooshed its way into the room again. None of the terrifying images accompanied the wind this time.

Cole ran both hands through his hair. "After that big breeze, I heard doors slamming—a lot of them. Then feet running above us. Blackbirds were dive-bombing the windows. Then a nurse fell, or heck, I don't know, jumped from a floor above this one. She fell and hit the edge. Blood and guts splashed everywhere. Then Laura Jean turned into a dead body."

Cynthia's eyes grew wide. "Jeez."

"Did the walls scream?" Kenny said.

Cole shook his head.

Cynthia's eyes widened. "Screaming walls?"

Kenny filled her in on their adventure last night. He didn't mention the part about seeing the Creeper.

"So that's what all that was about. You two were snooping?"

"I wasn't snooping. And it wasn't the screaming that woke me. I saw something."

Cole didn't know how to say it. He wasn't sure what he saw, after all.

"He thinks he saw the Creeper."

Cole cringed inwardly.

"You're pulling my leg," Cynthia said.

"Uh-uh, no. I heard a door open. There was someone standing out here, dressed in rags or something. The head was, I don't know, like a monster. It moved fast and the light was out."

Cynthia's eyebrows knitted together. The scars on her face became distorted in her confusion.

"The door to the dorm was open. It's never like that," Kenny reported. "Lights were out too. Have you ever seen that?"

"All right, you're scaring the crap out of me."

"It's the truth, I swear," Cole said.

"How come he isn't dead?" Cynthia asked Kenny.

Cole groaned and rubbed his hair again. Pressure was mounting, and he found himself thinking of the word heaven. He pictured the word, written in white on a blue background. He counted the letters, tracing each one in his mind. H-E-A-V-E-N. Six letters, all in caps. In the background he heard Kenny and Cynthia.

"I don't know. I don't get it either. Unless—" He drummed his fingers on his knee. "Unless that part isn't true. Or what he saw wasn't the Creeper."

"So you didn't see it?"

"Nah, whatever it was it was gone by the time I joined him."

The pressure was easing, but Cole counted the letters again just to make sure.

7

Timmy Wins H-O-R-S-E and Cole Gets Shocked

DALE CAME IN A LITTLE before noon. Cole felt relieved. The male nurse seemed pretty decent yesterday, and Kenny confirmed that was the case when Cole asked him. Some of the staff would've gone nuts about the out-of-bed incident last night, according to Kenny, but Dale was okay with it after his initial annoyance. Cole felt he could even overlook the fact that he snitched on them to Nurse Stern.

"We get to go outside with him a lot to play football or basketball. Beats sitting in this shithole all day."

That was welcome news. Although Cole wasn't the best at sports, he was okay enough. Anything to get them to go outside.

Kenny leaned over the arm of the couch and looked out the window. The haze was turning into puffy clouds. The tops were high enough that the underside was a threatening gray.

"We won't go out if it rains. Shit."

The clouds weren't organized yet. Patches of blue were abundant. "It'll rain, but it'll hold off until later."

Kenny smiled. Cynthia, who was kneeling on her haunches while playing solitaire on the floor, also glanced up.

"How do you know? You're a weatherman?" Kenny said.

An answer hit Cole right away. "Nope, I'm a seer."

Cynthia rolled her eyes and Kenny waved him off.

Timmy, however, giggled. "Cole made a funny."

Cole thought so too.

૬

When lunch came, Cole realized he was starving. The menu was simple—premade sandwiches of ham and cheese, egg salad, and peanut butter and jelly. Then there was milk and fruit cocktail.

Egg salad always looked and smelled like puke mixed with snot, so Cole avoided that. He had one PB&J and one ham sandwich. He asked Dale if he could have more, and Dale said sure. He had another ham and cheese. The milk was cold, so he had two glasses. Cole lost count, but he thought Kenny had three at least. Cynthia and Timmy only had one each. It was hard to tell what Beatrice had because she ground her food into a smooshed mess and ate it in chunks. Laura Jean had a tiny piece of ham without bread and no cheese. That was it. Cole didn't understand how she could live like that.

The radio was tuned to a top-hits station. "Johnny Angel" was playing. Cole liked the song and thought Shelley Fabares was pretty. He hummed along in his head.

"Cole is seeing ghosts." This came from Timmy to nobody in particular at the end of lunch before cleanup. Dale overheard the comment.

"Lots of patients claim to see ghosts." Dale leaned against a counter that contained the metal lunch containers that went to the kids' ward from the women's ward. "I've been here twenty years and never seen a single one."

"C'mon, Dale you must've seen something scary," Cynthia said.

Dale snorted. "Yeah. Patients."

A round of boos and snarky comments followed his reply.

"Not you guys," Dale said quickly. "You're all fine. There's been some adults, though, let me tell you. Speaking of scary, Cole, you've got dish-cleaning duty."

Cole had already seen the duty roster for the day and knew this was coming. Besides, he had helped Cynthia the previous night.

"Do you think you can handle it?"

Cole stood and gathered his plate. The other kids quickly stacked theirs on top of his until he had a tower of plastic plates. Within seconds, a pile of grimy plastic spoons and forks were added to the top.

"Yeah, I got it." He took the load carefully over to the sink to wash. Cynthia followed closely to grab a wet sponge to wipe down the tables. Meanwhile, Timmy resumed his comments to the rest of the room.

"Nineteen oh seven. That's when this opened. It was a boys' boarding school. Like a high school but you sleep there."

"How did you know that?" Cole called from the sink.

"From Lambert."

"That's right," Dale said while stacking some trays. "For about fifteen years. They were a powerhouse at football. Even played Tech and UVA. They recruited the biggest brutes from the area. Evidently they weren't the nicest kids."

"Ugh. I can't imagine a school full of football players."

These were the first words Cole had heard Laura Jean say to the whole group.

"I know, God. I couldn't stand it," Cynthia agreed.

"A couple died," Timmy said.

"What? You mean kids?" This from Kenny.

"Um. Two. Killed themselves."

"I never heard *that*," said Dale.

"One was a girl."

There was a chorus of *what*s.

"It was a boys' school," said Dale.

"I know. But the girl was a girlfriend of one of the boys. She had a baby. She jumped from the top floor. Or maybe the roof. She threw the baby off first."

That silenced the group. The only sound came from the radio. "Sherry" by the Four Seasons.

Cole felt like he'd been poked in the gut with the handle end of a baseball bat. He stepped away from the sink and back into the room. Soapsuds dripped from his fingertips.

Kenny and Cynthia stared at him. They looked as stunned as Cole felt. Why didn't Timmy say anything before? Timmy was a mystery, that's for sure.

"Is that true, Timmy?" Cole had to work up the nerve to ask the question. If it really happened, then he actually saw what he saw when he first arrived—and it would explain why the girl tossed her baby and then jumped.

"It's true. Lambert told me."

Cole was curious about Lambert and what else he knew.

"All right, you guys. Enough. You don't know if that's true. And Cole, you're dripping all over the floor."

Dale took everyone outside after the lunch chores were

completed. Before leaving, he grabbed a basketball from a supply closet within the nurses' station. Cynthia groaned when she saw the ball.

"Can I bring the transistor radio? It's too hot to play."

"Yes, and we'll play H-O-R-S-E so you won't get too sweaty."

There was a small basketball court on the side of the building where much of the recreation appeared to take place. Past that was a large field for touch football. A section of the field had four worn paths that made a diamond shape for softball.

Behind the building were rows of crops. Cole had learned from Kenny that the facility was actually a working farm for adult patients. Crops were sold in neighboring towns and provided fresh vegetables for hospital meals.

Not far from the farm, a back extension contained a small workout area. Chain-link fencing surrounded it. Barbed wire curled along the entire top of the fence. The setup made Cole uneasy.

"That's where they keep the crazy, violent people. We don't go near there. You don't want to be caught by any of those sick fuckers," Kenny said from behind as they gathered on the court.

Cole detected three men dressed in gray uniforms. Their skin was pale and reminded Cole of sour milk. They were staring at him with unblinking eyes. Cole felt a chill despite the swirling heat. If his demons ever took human form, he suspected they'd look a lot like these men.

"They're giving me the creeps," Cole said.

"No shit. C'mon, let's play."

As he turned away, Cole thought he saw one of them give him a wink.

Dale decided that Timmy would go first and set up the first challenge shot. Cole expected him to miss. He was surprised when Timmy called for a straightforward free throw—and made it with a swoosh of the net. He didn't hit the rim.

"Bet you didn't expect that," Kenny whispered.

Cole, Kenny, and also to his surprise, Cynthia made their free throws. Cole felt really nervous as he took his shot. It bounced twice on the rim before falling through. Laura Jean didn't want to play and just sat on the ground curled in a ball. Beatrice had no clue what was going on, but Dale got her to throw the ball underhanded once during the game. Otherwise, she just wandered around on the grass making noises.

Timmy's next shot was a layup. There was no bragging on his part. He just announced the shot and made it with little fanfare.

"He's pretty good," Cole said to Kenny.

"Yep. Nobody can figure out where he gets it. He doesn't say. Wait till we play football."

While Kenny and Cynthia made their shots, Cole missed his and collected an H, much to his humiliation. It was downhill from there. Timmy's challenges became increasingly difficult with each pass—from the sides, over the head, and over the head with eyes closed. Then it became crazy, involving twirls and special dribbling before shots. Cole missed everything and collected his O-R-S-E, the first to be eliminated. Cynthia made one additional shot but came up empty with all the others before she was gone.

Cole had to grudgingly admit that she was a decent shooter too.

Kenny hung in for a while before he had all the letters. Timmy won and, unlike any other kid, didn't gloat. He wanted to play again.

During their game, the sky had clouded up. Cole didn't notice until he thought he heard some distant thunder beyond the mountains.

"Dale, can I see you?"

Cole searched for the source of the voice and saw Nurse Stern along the sidewalk at the edge of the building.

"Be right there," Dale called. He turned to the kids. "Okay, everyone. Looks like we have to go in. A storm might be coming."

"Darn," Timmy said.

"It's no fun if you kick our asses all the time, man," Kenny said. "Save it for tomorrow."

"Hey, look." Cynthia pointed toward the field.

Beatrice ambled along a few yards away from them while staring at the grass. But that wasn't what Cynthia was referring to.

Well beyond Beatrice, a group of animals stood unmoving at the edge of the woods.

"Are those wolves?" Cynthia asked.

Cole focused at the skulk. "No, they're foxes. A bunch of them."

"Huh, they *are* foxes. I've never seen so many," Dale said.

"I've never seen *any*. You know about them?" Kenny asked Cole.

"A little from when I lived in the mountains with my nana."

The pack was staring at them. Or him, specifically. Overhead a flock of blackbirds called and flew in tightening circles.

Dale brought everyone to attention. "Let's start moving inside." He checked out the foxes one more time, then cupped his hands around his mouth and called loudly for Beatrice.

She lifted her head and loped toward the group. Dale looked relieved.

As the group made the turn from the side to the front of the building, they almost ran into Nurse Stern. Cynthia let out a little yelp of surprise, to which Nurse Stern smiled.

"Sorry, dear. I didn't mean to startle you." Only her lips curled upward.

Cole noticed Lambert picking some weeds from among the planted flowers along the front of the building. The old man seemed to register Cole's presence at the same time. He stood and bestowed on Cole a smile that was light years more genuine than Nurse Stern's.

"Hello, Cole. How's it been going?"

Cole paused and let Laura Jean and Beatrice slip around him. He wasn't surprised when Kenny and Cynthia stopped by Cole. Timmy did, too, but he stayed a number of steps away.

Nurse Stern was involved in a lengthy conversation with Dale. They weren't watching them or listening.

"It's been weird." That was the best way Cole could describe his first twenty-four hours.

The white hair on Lambert's deep brown skin looked like a day-old snowfall. Cole almost expected it to slide off in the heat as if it were melting. Lambert nodded multiple times as if he knew all about Cole's experience so far at Saint Edwards.

"Stranger than when you saw the leaper?"

Cole blew air forcefully past his lips in a dramatic sigh. "Yeah, I've seen a bunch of things." He didn't know how much he should go into it.

Kenny nudged him in the back with his elbow. "Go on, tell him."

Lambert raised his eyebrows and waited.

"Oh, man. It's hard to describe. I saw the walls scream, a nurse jump off the roof or out a window upstairs from us, there was slamming doors and running, and then..." Cole looked around. Laura Jean was waiting for the group on the front steps of the main entrance, out of earshot. "Then I saw Laura Jean turn into a dead body."

Lambert stood up straight and inhaled deeply. "My, son, you have been busy."

"That's not how I want to be."

"Understandable."

Cole remembered lunch. "Timmy said that the girl who threw the baby and herself off the roof was a girlfriend of one of the boys who used to go to school here. When it was a school, I mean."

Lambert looked thoughtful. "That's true. He got that from me. This was way back around the turn of the century. This young lady somehow appeared in town with a baby in her arms. She walked a long way carrying that child, let me tell you. One of the boys here was that baby's father. She was bound and determined to make that boy marry her. Treat her like a true lady. And become a rightful father for the baby."

Cole felt sorry for the girl and he didn't even know her. "It didn't work?"

"No. The boy refused to even talk to her. Said she was a whore and stormed away to his dorm room. An ugly scene for sure."

A rumble of thunder bounced its way along the nearer mountains.

"She was beside herself, and the headmaster couldn't shut the door on the poor girl, so he invited her in while he made arrangements for her to stay somewhere in town. While he talked with an assistant about possibilities, she stole her way up to the roof. And, well, you saw what happened."

"That's sad," Cynthia said.

"It is."

"What about the other leaper?" Kenny asked.

"Yeah," Cole said. "Did that many people jump?"

Lambert placed a hand on Cole's shoulder. "This place has a long, cruel history. Some of the stories I know. Some I can only guess at. Like you I just see what's happened. Or what happened afterwards."

The discussion between Nurse Stern and Dale had broken up. They were walking toward them. Dale looked a little troubled. Nurse Stern seemed pleased. Maybe they'd had a disagreement and she won.

"Looks like you're headed in," Lambert said to their small gathering. He turned to Cole. "You're sensitive to seeing leapers. Lord knows why. Dead is dead at the end of the day."

"Lambert, it seems like you should be getting inside, too," Nurse Stern said.

"Yes, ma'am. That rain sure is moving in. My flowers will be happy. They're thirsty." He stepped back to let Nurse Stern by him and up the steps.

"Let's go to the ward now," Dale announced. "Walk. No running."

"Yes, Dad," Kenny said.

Nurse Stern gave him a look.

"Don't be a smart aleck. Cole? Everyone except you. You need to go with Nurse Stern."

Lightning momentarily brightened the darkening sky. Seconds went by before the thunder cascaded angrily.

"But, why?" Cole felt like the lightning had struck him.

"Come now, Cole. Dr. Slaver would like to see you. You'll rejoin your friends later."

Uneasy, Cole followed her up the steps. Fat raindrops began falling. They were moments away from a downpour. From behind, a hand lightly touched Cole's neck. He turned to see Lambert. His face was drawn.

"Be brave, son. You'll be fine. Just fine."

Cole couldn't help feeling that Lambert didn't believe his own words.

The first indication that something was wrong came when they went downstairs to the basement instead of to the doctor's office, which was on the fourth floor.

The stairs to the basement were directly under the ornate staircase on the first floor but not as attractive. The walls were painted a mucous-colored green and the floors were dingy linoleum. When Cole reached the bottom of the steps, the hallway went in both directions. To the right he saw Daniel, the maintenance guy. He was carrying a stepladder and light-bulbs.

"Hello there, little man," Daniel said, his voice joyful. Behind Daniel and farther down the hall came a rumbling sound. Cole knew what it was right away. A big dryer or maybe a couple of dryers. He remembered Daniel with the laundry cart yesterday. The man probably did laundry every day.

"Hi," Cole said in return, although his voice was weak from nerves.

"This way, Cole," Nurse Stern said and directed him to the left.

Right before turning to follow the nurse in the opposite

direction, Cole noticed a dark entryway at the end of the hall beyond the operating dryers. It was pitch black and spooky and almost looked like a tunnel. Oddly enough, there was a metal gate in front of the entrance that reminded him of the collapsible gates on old-fashioned elevators. Cole could see a big padlock on the gate. Why it was kept locked?

"Cole?"

He tore his head from the direction of tunnel. Nurse Stern stood ramrod straight, her hands clasped over her belly. She wasn't carrying her clipboard.

The left-side hallway was empty but lit with two rows of florescent lights. The walls were painted the yellow of sunflower petals. No pictures hung the entire length. Midway down the wall, cream-colored tiles went to the floor. The entire passage was ugly.

"Follow me, please." Nurse Stern's face was like a cold statue. She turned without waiting and walked down the center of the hallway, white shoes squeaking on the floor.

Cole swallowed involuntarily and trailed the nurse.

The feeling of his demons escalated. They had been lying low, but their activity seemed to explode around him in an instant. He counted his steps, hoping to end on an even one.

Despite being vacant, the corridor was full of murmuring sounds. Cole searched for the source but could only see an empty wooden chair at the end of the hall. A closed door came up quickly on the left.

An engraved sign read *Surgery*.

Cole felt chilled for a reason he couldn't explain. What was he doing here?

The demons revved up their attack. He could almost sense them gathering behind his back, ready to pounce. His heart pounded in his chest.

They walked past the surgical room and headed for the next door, outside of which sat the wooden chair.

"Sit here for one moment, Cole."

Seventeen steps. The demons were winning.

Cole sat, and Nurse Stern turned the knob of the door and entered. As the door swung open, the sounds of voices amplified.

So this was where the talkers were.

The chair was hard and not particularly comfortable. Cole so much wanted to stand and run away. Something didn't *feel* right. He counted tiles, all the while tracing the rectangular shapes on this thumb using his index finger. Four sides. Four. Even.

The engraved sign on this door read *Treatment Room*.

What kind of treatment? And, more importantly, was this for him?

He counted the letters in *treatment*. There were nine.

Cole felt a jolt of lightheadedness. It came on so quickly that he thought he might fall out of the chair. Grabbing the armrests, he squeezed his eyes shut—and was bombarded with an image of Timmy screaming on a long table with a padded green surface.

Cole flinched. When he opened his eyes, the image wouldn't leave. He saw Timmy on the table kicking and swinging his arms. His body fought and arched while he tried to escape a group of people who surrounded the table. A nurse he didn't know practically threw herself on top of him. A big guy in a white uniform tightened leather straps around his shins and then his thighs. Another nurse caught his right arm and fastened it to the table. Someone got the left and did the same. Finally his chest was wrapped in the straps.

Timmy kept howling. There might've been words in the screams, but Cole couldn't make them out. The entire scene was horrifying.

"Cole?" Nurse Stern had opened the door.

Cole flinched again.

The image of Timmy's screams disappeared with a loud pop in his brain. Nurse Stern gave no indication that she heard the noise. The tiniest of cries escaped his lips.

"No reason to be afraid, Cole. You'll be just fine. Come in." She backtracked into the room and held the door open. "We want to help you get rid of those scary hallucinations you have."

For a sheer moment, Cole thought of turning on his heels and taking off. But where would he go? They'd only catch him and he'd end up screaming like Timmy.

As he entered the room, he saw the same green table. Surrounding it was the same group of people that had been with Timmy. The large man in the white uniform, two nurses, and Dr. Slaver.

"Go on, Cole." Nurse Stern firmly guided him into the room with a hand on the base of his neck.

One of the other nurses smiled a little. She patted the table to indicate he should climb up.

Cole didn't think he could move. His arms and legs were shaking. His fingers tingled. The sight of Timmy shrieking had unnerved him so much. He swallowed and took a step. He didn't fall. He took another.

"Come on, son." This from Dr. Slaver. His bulging eyes and puffy lips made him look like a goldfish. His eyes were filmy, and Cole observed dried discharge in both corners. He felt queasy.

Cole reached the table and touched the green surface.

It was padded, which he hadn't anticipated. Attached to the underside were the leather straps.

They were going to tie him down. Fasten him so he couldn't move.

For some stupid reason, Bruce's comment came to mind. *I hope they shock your brains out.*

Oh God.

"Are you going to shock me?"

"Sit on up here now." Dr. Slaver again. He seemed impatient.

"Are you?"

"Cole, you're a big boy. You'll do fine. You won't even feel it." Nurse Stern twirled him around by the shoulders. Her guidance was gentle but no-nonsense.

Somehow, Cole hoisted himself up to the table.

"Scoot back, now," the nurse who'd smiled at him said.

Cole scooted. The same pleasant nurse touched his chest and gently guided him down to the table. Cole looked at her, inwardly willing her to let him go. "Please." It came out as a whisper. She averted her eyes and reached for a strap on her side.

The others were busy. The big guy was briskly attaching the straps around his legs and his ankles. Cole raised his head and saw that the man's face was scarred with pockmarks. A brown mole on one cheek had hairs growing out of it. The straps on Cole's ankles were tight to the point of hurting, but the man didn't seem to care.

Dr. Slaver and Nurse Stern talked softly behind his head. He couldn't follow what they were saying.

The nurse on his opposite side tied something to his upper arm and followed this with a couple of slaps to the inside of his elbow with her fingers. "I'm looking for a good vein," she said, probing. "And I found one." She made it sound like this was great news.

Nurse Stern's face appeared above his upside down. "We're going to give you two kinds of medicine before we start. The first is a muscle relaxant, and then we'll put you to sleep. You won't feel the shock at all."

A needle slid into his vein with a pinch. Rubber tubing was attached to a bag that hung on a pole. The nurse took a syringe and gave him a shot.

The walls began screaming. Faces pushed out behind the paint. More than he could count. The screams were similar to Timmy's, but somehow worse. There were sounds of dead branches long fallen from trees, splitting and cracking.

Outside, thunder boomed. The lights flickered briefly.

"Let's move this along before we lose electricity," Dr. Slaver said.

Cole began to feel like rubber. The screaming faces calmed down and shrunk back into the plaster.

A tongue depressor was used to apply a cool, wet gel to his temples.

"Tilt your head back." This might've been Nurse Stern. He could no longer tell. The room was floating far away. A hand cupped his chin.

"Open your mouth." Something made of rubber was placed in his mouth. "You can bite on this."

The room faded.

8

The Leaper and the Creeper

A NURSE LOOKED DOWN AT him.

"There you are." She smiled while she was fussing with something out of his view. He heard a belt being unbuckled on his left. Then the nurse leaned over him and made some additional moves with her hands on his right side.

Where was he?

The nurse moved down to his feet and made additional motions followed by more unbuckling. Cole found that he could move his arms. He realized he couldn't before.

Before? Before what? His head hurt and his stomach kind of gurgled.

Cole tried to sit up but couldn't.

"Easy," the nurse said. She had returned to a position by his head. "You'll be a little groggy and confused for a while.

I still have you strapped in along your waist so you don't fall off the table."

"What...where?"

"Shush now. You rest a little bit more. I won't leave you." The nurse wiped his face with a cool, damp cloth. "You know, you have the prettiest eyes."

Sometime later, and he wasn't clear how much later, he opened his eyes.

"Hello." The room was empty.

"Good, you're back." This came from behind. A nurse, the same one as before, appeared at his side. "Would you like to sit up?"

Cole nodded. He pushed himself up by his hands. The room spun and he gagged.

"Easy, take it slow. Deep breaths."

Cole took deep breaths but otherwise didn't move. His feet were still on the table and his knees were up. His hands remained behind him, propping him up.

"Slow your breathing. There you go. Try scooting back to the edge where your feet are." The nurse spoke softly.

Moving ever so slowly, Cole pushed with his hands and slid his butt down the table. When he couldn't go any farther, he slid his feet down. Cole looked at his socks and wondered vaguely where his sneakers were. Had he even been wearing them?

With his feet over the edge, Cole pushed again until he felt a stool under his toes. He was able to sit up straight. Again the room swirled, but he didn't retch.

"Sit there for a bit and get your bearings."

The rotating sensation stopped and Cole took the chance to look around. The nurse was retrieving something from under a chair.

"Dale brought Kenny down here when they went to get dinner. Kenny thought you'd like your slippers. They took your sneakers upstairs."

"Thanks."

Flashes were coming back to him. Playing H-O-R-S-E outside. A storm coming. Following Nurse Stern down...down here.

Cole looked around again. The straps on the table. Thoughts of Timmy screaming. Another table behind him. A contraption on the table with dials and knobs.

"Did I get shocked?"

The nurse stepped in front of him and gently placed her hands on his shoulders. "Yes, honey, you did. And you did very well."

"I don't remember."

"No. And you won't. You were put to sleep."

That explained it.

"I need to ask you some questions before we leave," the nurse said.

Cole returned her gaze and waited.

"What's your name?"

"Cole."

"Cole what?"

"Nightshade."

"Excellent." The nurse grinned.

"Where are you?"

"In the basement."

She chuckled. "I mean, where are you...?" She spread her arms and looked all around her.

"Oh. Um." Cole had to think. "The mental asylum." Cole concentrated further. *Edward.* No, no...then he had it. "Saint Edwards." He smiled. Getting it right felt good.

"Okay, last one. When's your birthday."

Cole grinned a little more. "Today."

"Very good. Sometimes when people go through this, they forget things. Don't worry if it happens. Everything comes back in a day or so. But you seem to be doing pretty good."

"People forget their names?"

"Only for a short while. Let's have you step down now." She took his elbow and helped him. "Careful. Can you slip your slippers on?" Cole did. "We're going to walk upstairs to the unit. We'll take it slow. They saved some dinner for you."

"What time is it?" They walked into the hallway. Now he recalled the yucky yellow and cream colors.

"It's about seven or seven thirty."

"Really?"

The walk to the stairwell took forever. As they approached, he heard footfalls on the steps. Kenny bounded into view, followed shortly by Dale.

"There you are," Dale said. "We thought we'd come down to carry you upstairs so Nurse Jennings can get home."

Even though Cole was lightheaded, he was glad to see them. Especially Kenny.

"Thanks you, guys. I'll let you take him, then."

Kenny turned his back to Cole and squatted down in front of him. "Here. Climb on. I'll give you a piggyback ride."

"Easy," both nurses said.

Cole climbed on Kenny's back. He almost slipped off, but Kenny brought his arms under his legs. Cole clutched him around the neck. Kenny smelled like sweat and the outdoors. Cole thought it was great.

"We're going," Kenny announced and walked toward the stairs.

"We're following you two. Be careful."

Cole heard the nurses behind him. When the pleasant nurse split off from them on the first floor, she said, "Goodnight, Cole."

Cole mumbled in reply. Riding on Kenny's back was making him drowsy. By the time they reached the kids' ward on the second floor, he was dozing off.

♆

"You're going to feel strange for another day or so," Dale said while helping him undress for bed.

"Great," Cole muttered. He swayed as he T-shirt came off. Dale gently lowered him to the bed. Over Dale's shoulder, Kenny and Timmy watched. While Kenny didn't seem bothered by Cole's state, Timmy was biting his lip.

Since he'd returned to his ward about half an hour ago, Cole felt in no shape to sit up for long periods, let alone carry on conversations.

He'd dozed off while chewing a sandwich, which upset Cynthia for some reason. "Cole," she hissed, and tapped her knuckles on the table. He woke with a start to finish the sandwich, but that was all he could accomplish. Dale came over and said, *Let's go to bed, kiddo.*

And here they were.

He lay back when he slid his pants down. Dale tossed them aside by the T-shirt.

"You might sleep a lot tomorrow, too. No big deal. I won't be here, by the way. I'm taking the day off. Peggy comes in later, and she'll be here tomorrow with Roy. He'll take care of you."

Behind Dale, Kenny rolled his eyes.

"Medication time, you two. Come on, let him get some rest."

Timmy filed out behind Dale, still biting his lip. Kenny hesitated for a second. "See you later," he said, and left.

The sobs were heartbreaking.

Cole couldn't figure out the source. He walked to the common room and even down the girls' hallway. The girls had individual rooms with little windows. He looked, feeling guilty for doing so, but he couldn't help it. Lumps under bedsheets were the only thing visible.

He sighed. This was going nowhere. The volume of the sobbing remained the same wherever he went.

Back in the common room, the lights were off. A desk lamp was lit in the nurses' station that cast enough light into the common room for Cole to see. No nurse, though. Where was Dale? He was on duty till midnight. Was it later than that? He couldn't find a clock to check.

The sobbing got louder. Cole spun his head, searching. The anguish was horrible to hear.

There.

Aha. Coming up the stairs outside the ward.

He ran to the door and pulled it open. Wait, wasn't it supposed to be kept locked at night?

Cole stepped into the corridor. A girl carrying a baby was coming up the stairs. She reached his level and looked right through him. How come she didn't see him?

The girl said "Stairs" to herself in between her sobs. She searched the floor and found the next staircase a few yards down the hall. She headed in that direction.

The baby in her arms was quiet, as if the girl was doing all the crying for both of them.

"Are you okay?" Cole said.

She ignored him or never heard him.

Cole trotted to catch up to her. "Hey." He reached his hand to touch the elbow not holding the baby and felt nothing. He tried again. Nothing. There was no form.

Cole shuddered. "Hey, please. What're you doing?"

She mounted the steps. Cole followed in her wake and kept within arm's length. At the landing halfway up to the next floor she picked up speed. Cole was unprepared for her burst of energy and tried to take off after her. He couldn't run. It was like he was trying to force his way through deep snow.

The girl reached the third floor and disappeared down the hall.

"Wait!"

Cole somehow burst his way through the invisible mire.

"For God's sake, stop." Cole had realized who the girl was and what she was going to do. "You can't do this."

He yelled after her, a sound that expressed his distress but not the words.

He found that he could sprint and discovered her tracks to the next staircase. She was disappearing onto the floor when he reached the landing. He took the steps two at a time.

The hall was dark and no rooms were visible.

"Hello?"

Second door. Second door on your left.

Nana? That was Nana.

How did she get here?

A doorframe marked the first door. He slid the palm of his hand along the wall and walked briskly. Where was it? Where was the door?

The hallway was taking forever. It shouldn't be this long to the next room.

Fingertips slammed painfully into the frame.

Here.

His hands scrambled, feeling for the doorknob. He couldn't find it.

Push.

He pushed. The door opened and sunlight exploded into the hallway. Cole fell back instinctively from the glare.

Recovering his balance, he squinted until his pupils adjusted.

The girl stood before an open window. The baby was propped on her hip. A small fist was shoved into his mouth.

"No. You can't do this."

The girl didn't acknowledge him. Cole understood at last that she couldn't hear or see him.

"There's nothing you can do."

Cole spun around. Dale leaned against a wall, inspecting his fingernails.

"This is just a dream. Save yourself the aggravation and stay where you are."

The girl wailed and startled Cole into looking back. She lifted the baby, kissed his cheek, and casually tossed him out the open window. Just like that. A heartbeat later, she climbed onto the windowsill and dove off.

Cole moaned in response. His feet moved toward the window. He knew he'd regret seeing her smashed again on the concrete below, but there was no stopping him.

"I wouldn't do that if I were you." Dale's voice behind him was fading as if he was walking away. Cole kept going.

The window was wider than it looked from the doorway. He was able to plant his hands on the sill and lean out.

The girl and her baby were not at the bottom.

Instead, there were two other bodies. One was Cynthia.

And one was Timmy. They had been smashed and splattered on the main steps below. Their streams of blood ran together and mixed as they flowed down the steps.

🦋

Cole gasped and sat up in bed. He swung his feet over the side.

Kenny was sound asleep in his bed. His breathing was deep and relaxed. Across the way, Timmy turned over and made noises but quickly settled.

Cole eased back down. The bottom sheet was damp. He felt sweat across his chest and back. The windows were still open and the air was damp, but a little cooler. The earlier rain had stopped.

"You've been out a long time."

Nana stood on the side of his bed opposite from Kenny. Cole wasn't surprised that she'd showed up.

"I know. It's been strange."

"You saw the girl jump. How sad."

Yes, he had to admit it was.

"Remember, child, what I've always said. You're like a radio receiver. You capture the radio waves that are always around. But you've got to be tuned to the right signal to catch them. You haven't learned to tune away from these signals or turn off the radio. So you keep catching these waves. You're going to tune into some sad things. Some nasty things. Some may not like for you to listen in and some will not care. You just need to learn and protect yourself when the time comes."

Nana often talked like this, but that didn't make it any easier to understand.

"Listen now, child. What do you hear?"

Cole tuned in as best he could. At first there was nothing.

Then there were screams and moans. Souls were wailing all over the asylum. Kids cried here—just like his visions of Timmy. Then the flash of an image: Cole saw some kids curled up in a ball, rocking and sobbing.

On the floor above. More cries. This time they weren't kids. But ladies. Women. Their howls were devastating. Cole felt all happiness and joy being sucked out of his soul. What could make these women feel so miserable?

Then, on the basement floor and other floors—especially the added building out back, came the screams of men. Howls of desperation and pain. But there was more. There was anger. And rage.

Footsteps ran through the corridors. Furniture smashed. Doors slammed.

Cole covered his ears. "Nana! Make it stop. God, it's awful."

It stopped. Nana looked pained.

"Nana. When did this all happen?"

"Oh, child. This place has been here for years and years. These things have been happening since the day the building opened as a school. They got worse when it turned into an asylum. They'll continue as long as the place is here and terrible people live within its walls."

Cole shut his eyes tight. "Nana…" Cole didn't know what he was going to ask. He opened his eyes and turned to her.

But Nana was gone.

Later.

Cole was on his stomach. His head ached a little. His mouth was dry.

Rough feeling fingertips touched his right calf. He wanted

to turn over, but he was paralyzed. His muscles disobeyed every command he gave.

The fingers lifted, and he hoped the person had gone. But no. They returned and touched his back. One finger traced designs on his skin.

"So beautiful." Barely a whisper.

Oh God.

The hands grasped his shoulders and slowly flipped him over. There wasn't any noise.

Cole looked up.

Kenny! Timmy!

The Creeper looked down at him.

The monster's fingers were dry like sandpaper. It clasped its hands on Cole's sides and pinched his skin.

"You'll do nicely," the thing hissed.

Slices of skin hung loosely from the Creeper's skull. Its arms and belly, too. A slight breeze tumbled through the screen and the pieces of skin rippled.

In the next bed, Kenny shifted position.

The creature coiled, ready to strike Kenny.

Nothing happened. Kenny snored a few times and fell silent.

The Creeper backed away silently, like a ghost.

Later still.

Cole thought he was dreaming. There were sounds nearby that didn't make sense. He was on his side, and he opened his eyes and looked in Kenny's direction. Kenny was moving up and down. His sheets were off. He was naked.

Beneath him was someone. Breathing and moaning. Kenny kept moving.

Afterward, a hint of dawn filtered into the dorm.

There was enough light to see Nurse Peggy stand, button her blouse, and smooth out her skirt.

Cole dozed.

"How're you doing, Cole?" Kenny was sitting up in his bed. His underwear was back on. The room was lighter, so that meant it was later. Timmy was still asleep.

The night had been hell. He'd tossed and turned and had the most awful dreams. If they were dreams.

"I feel like crap."

"Oh, sorry. You'll feel okay later." Kenny stretched out again on his bed.

Cole slept.

9

Chaz Captures Shirley Temple

CHAZ REALLY GOT OFF ON this stuff. Always had and, he hoped, always would. He'd graduated from college the previous May with a useless combination of an American history major and a film studies minor. What he really wanted to pursue was a lucrative research program into the paranormal. Hell, it didn't even need to be lucrative. As long as it paid the bills and, well, got him laid. Which was proving to be difficult. He didn't have much cash and he was still living with his parents.

"Son, don't you think it's about time you gave up on this ghost infatuation?" This was the most frequently asked question by his father, bar none. Some variation of it had begun in high school and continued ever since. The less-than-subtle hints about growing up and abandoning childish interests were always being tossed around. Chaz had the misfortune of being the third and last child in his family. One of his sisters was in med school, and the other one was an engineer. They'd studied the "hard sciences," as his mother mentioned at every opportunity.

Chaz plugged away at his long-term goal anyway. When he was much younger, the message he'd received from his parents had always been to follow your heart, do what you like as long as you're happy. They'd never expected he'd gravitate toward this territory. He and some college buddies had dabbled in ghost hunting with certified "experts" (assholes, really) while in school. These guys were clueless. They became enamored with the TV shows and shot their wads trying to become famous. Needless to say, they didn't succeed.

Chaz developed a plan to conduct his investigations in a scholarly manner: collect data, organize the data, compare similarities across haunted sites, you name it. Chaz had ideas. He finessed social media to develop a following and learned from people he thought were legitimate. His blogs were informative and demanding in terms of rigor. He could see a book, maybe several books, in his future. A YouTube channel, even. And then who knew what could happen.

The one minor catch was money. Or lack thereof.

Eventually he interviewed with Rutledge for this gig. Rutledge was charmed by his enthusiasm and gave him the job. Okay, it was a glorified tour guide at minimum pay. But hell, he was making connections. And Saint Edwards had definite possibilities as a location for him to make a name for himself. Rutledge was supportive—after all if Chaz struck gold, Rutledge would benefit.

Working with Evie was also a huge plus. She was fun. Most of the girls he'd met with an interest in the paranormal, and he acknowledged that this was a limited sample, were pudgy with blue hair and nose rings. Even if sex with Evie was off the table, her existence gave him hope for hot girls in the future.

"There've been multiple reports of ghosts and other eerie occurrences in and outside the women's ward," Chaz said, taking over from Evie. He circled the perimeter of the crowd to face the front of the group. He flashed his best smile toward the three wives, exposing his orthodontic-straightened teeth. Chaz posed in a way that accentuated his shoulders and flat stomach. He'd been working out vigorously since college and was making a point to decrease his consumption of fast-food crap. The wives rewarded him with bright smiles and a quick scan of his body.

The tour garb was actually better than decent. Short-sleeved, dark-red polo shirts, with "St. Edwards Asylum" embroidered in the front upper-left side, were well made and fit comfortably. These "uniform" shirts, along with khakis—long pants or shorts, depending on the temperature—were regular wear for the guides. These very shirts, plus tee versions, were available in the gift shop. Rutledge left nothing to chance.

"The most common hauntings have been walking and running footsteps in the ward and outside in the hall. Many have characterized the footsteps as panicked or desperate. In addition, disembodied screams and voices have been heard."

"What's disembodied?" The middle kid asked.

Evie jumped in. "That's where there're voices that aren't attached to a person. Or a body. So, a sound lacking a physical source."

"Aha. A ghost, then." The Beard.

"That's what we think," Chaz said.

Behind Chaz on a shelf was a digital remote. He picked it

up, being careful not to overextend the curled cord that was secured to the wall. The cord actually had a lot of give, but Chaz wanted to make this operation look smooth.

"But it's not all footsteps and screams."

He pointed the remote at a twenty-four-inch digital frame hanging on a wall. The frame turned on, ready to initiate a slideshow. The crowd turned en masse for the demonstration.

"We've got four pictures in this slideshow," he said. "The first gives you an idea of what the ward looked like before the renovation."

The slide appeared. The shot was of the common room, where they were standing. Spray-painted scribbles slashed the walls in an angry pattern. Pieces of furniture littered the ground. Chunks of plaster had been knocked out of the walls, one in particular. Chaz imagined it had been done with a sledgehammer. The floor seemed grimy, as if there had been a flood, and dried silt was all that remained after the water receded. What accounted for that coating of dirt, he had no idea.

At the ten-second mark, the picture faded to black and a new one appeared. Chaz paused the display.

While the image of the ward in disarray set the stage, this was intended as a grab-you-by-the-throat shot and frequently worked as such. It did with this group.

A few faint gasps initially, but then the inevitable closer steps toward the frame. Happened every time.

"Is that…?" Potbelly.

"I'll be. That's convincing," The dad said.

"Is that a lady?" One of the kids asked.

"That *is* creepy," said one of the college girls. The one who didn't talk clutched her friend's arm. Chaz had his own image flash before his eyes: him in bed with both of them.

Stay focused.

"That picture was snapped by a team of paranormal investigators back when the owner purchased the property," Chaz said, and let that sink in for a moment. "And yes, it certainly appears to be a young woman kneeling on the floor in the common room. Right where we're standing."

Heads turned, looking for the perspective of the photographer and the location of where the figure had been kneeling.

"Kneeling?" Baldy and his wife asked simultaneously.

Pretty cool. They were getting into it.

"Watch this GIF," Chaz said. He hit the play button. A short looped sequence began on the screen. The start showed the young woman stationary. She stood up in a manner that suggested she had been kneeling. Then she disappeared. The loop repeated after a few seconds.

"Oh, man."

"Jeez."

Multiple gasps.

Someone shrieked.

A perfect reaction from the crowd. Chaz smiled and searched out Evie. He winked at her. She smiled back.

The old dude hung back, not leaning forward like everyone else. One of the wives saw this and turned in his direction.

"Would you like a closer look?"

"I'm fine, thank you." The old dude bowed slightly in appreciation. "I can see from here. Impressive."

"It is, isn't it," the woman said. "I'm not sure how real it is, but still."

Chaz smiled inwardly. Common reactions once again. They were hooked for the rest of the tour. He could feel it.

When the buzz died down, Chaz knew it was time to move to the next slide.

"This was also taken by the paranormal investigators."

The group's jitters vanished as appreciative oohs and aahs bubbled up. The second screen showed a corridor, the one to the east, which they'd stroll down in a few moments. A translucent figure in a long dress or bathrobe stood dead center at the end of the hall. The image was fuzzy and looked fake to Chaz, like a double exposure from the old-fashioned film days. Or something photoshopped.

"Does this one move?" This from one of the kids. The middle one. He was quite talkative.

"No. This is just a photo," Evie offered.

Chaz almost added, *And not a convincing one at that.*

The image faded to black. No need to wait for the ten-second rotation.

The last photo showed the same corridor. What made it eerie was a head sticking out of a doorframe as if the person was peering into the hallway. The head had long, tightly curled hair. On it was a huge bow. It looked like something a little girl would wear.

Chaz waited. Not for the typical gasp this time, but to see whether someone would provide a name.

Nobody knew who she really was, but when Rutledge first saw the picture, he practically roared. "My God. Was Shirley Temple a patient here?"

Evie had joined in with his laughter, as did some of the other staff. Chaz, who had no freaking idea who that was, feigned amusement and googled the person later. When he saw the childhood pictures of the actress, he understood.

"Shirley Temple." This was the old dude. Typically, it was people of a certain age who saw the resemblance.

"For heaven's sake. You're right. It does look like her," Baldy's wife said. Then came the inevitable brief conversation about who the heck Shirley Temple was for the benefit of the unenlightened and the young.

When the magical moment came for the big reveal, Chaz announced, "I took this picture."

They wanted the story, of course. Chaz had everyone's attention after the group twisted around as one to face him. He couldn't help smiling at the reaction, but customers never seemed to mind. The college girls were right smack in front. They positively beamed at him, and he so much wanted to taste their lip gloss.

"Okay, kid. Don't hold back now," the Beard said, looking amused. And impressed, Chaz thought.

Chaz had just gotten the job and was doing research. He read whatever history and reports were available on Saint Edwards, including an article with photos in a regional magazine. He even found chronicles of treatments and day-to-day logs in storage describing attempts at insulin-shock therapy, water treatments, electroconvulsive therapy, and early uses of medication like Thorazine. Some of these things were absolutely ghastly to read about.

The ghost stories hadn't been officially recorded but were gathered from journals, diaries, and oral histories from former employees and patients.

In addition to reading as many accounts as he could get his hands on, Chaz took multiple tours within the asylum. Evie accompanied him on some, others were self-guided. The latter allowed Chaz to experience the atmosphere on his own, and he made good use of the encounters. He audio-recorded his thoughts and took pictures constantly.

"There was an occasion earlier in June when I was in here by myself. It was nice out, warm but low humidity. These wards can get kind of oppressive when the humidity is high.

I'm not sure how the patients could stand it. Or the staff. Anyway, on that day it was as close to perfect as it can get.

"It was late afternoon when I entered the ward. I didn't walk through any of the other locations. Something told me to come to this floor."

Chaz was prepping for a tour later that evening. The final touches on the areas already renovated were just about done. The full slate of tours would begin next week once school was out and more families would be on the road. He and Evie were working on updates to their script, and they both thought that talking about their personal experiences with the place would make it feel more authentic.

The women's ward was open, as all the wards were. Doors were locked only for security purposes at the end of the day— and of course prior to the beginning of a tour to capture the claustrophobic feel of an asylum with the slap of a deadbolt.

The late-afternoon sun was lazy in the common room, which faced north. No bright rays or crisp shadows, only the gentle indirect light. The dining room was a different story. Blazing rays lit upon the empty tables and institutional chairs. Chaz felt it was too intense and would've preferred window shades. Rutledge was taking suggestions from his employees about what type, but Chaz couldn't help there. He'd never considered that there might be different kinds.

Rutledge had asked him to scout out decent locations for the digital frames that were going to be hung. He'd been making a few mental notes on the possibilities. Regardless of whether the dining room received any shades, it would still be too bright. The best spot for the digital frame would be in the common room.

And they needed pictures for that.

Luckily, they already had the GIF and the photo from

the paranormal investigators. Still, he and Evie were always taking shots with their cell phones whenever they were in the wards. They often did the same at night, after the tours ended, as they went around and locked down the facility. Who knew when they might get lucky?

Chaz went down the east corridor. He stopped at each room and checked it out. Some of the rooms had old wooden bedframes and stained mattresses on display. Others were empty.

Hey.

Chaz stopped. He'd heard that. He really did.

Hey.

He had just taken his head out of a doorway when the single word was spoken. It had the sound of an exhalation of breath.

Chaz stood stock still. He emptied his mind and listened. The clicks and plinks of random noise echoed in his ears. Nothing else, though. He scanned the doorways in front of him and searched for any unearthly shadows. Again, nothing.

But he could definitely sense something. A presence.

Chaz wasn't scared by any means. He was excited. Thrilled, actually. So he waited.

Just when he thought nothing else would happen, and more than a little disappointed as a result, he felt something on his face. The slightest rub on his cheek with gentle finger-tips. A pat on the top of his head and a delicate smoothing of his hair. Chaz was reminded of his mother doing the same thing when he was a little kid. The imagery came to him with a profound clarity.

Then the presence, or ghost or whatever, was gone.

Chaz took a few steps backward, raised his phone, and snapped multiple pictures.

"I really wanted to hurry out of the ward to see if I caught anything. But I knew I had to continue with my personal tour. The experience was amazing, and I was thinking maybe there'd be more. But unfortunately, nothing else happened."

The group watched him intently. One of the college girls had her hands folded in front of her face.

"I texted Evie. Turns out she was just downstairs in the lobby. When I found her, we checked out the pictures together."

"I couldn't believe it when I saw the shot," Evie said, contributing her perspective. "The first two or three showed nothing but hallway. Then all of a sudden, this." She pointed to the digital frame.

"Did you think it was the "Shirley Temple" ghost who touched you?" the old dude asked.

"I was wondering the same thing," the Potbelly's wife said.

"I don't know," Chaz said. "It could've been. The touch was gentle—something a mother would do." He looked at Mom and she smiled. Two of her kids were looking up at her.

"In any case, we don't know who she is. Or was." Chaz shrugged.

The few in the group chatted among themselves. Others turned to look at the photo again. Chaz gave them a couple of moments to collect themselves. Evie nodded to him.

"Okay, we can take a walk down the hallways. I'll show you were I was standing when I felt the caress. And where I took the picture."

10

Lambert Provides the Lay of the Land

September 1962

COLE DID FEEL BETTER WHEN he woke.

The sun was shining and the dorm room was bathed in brilliant sunshine. The breeze coming in through the open windows was still warm, but not hot and muggy like it had been. It was later than usual, too. The shadows were different in the room, which meant the sun was higher in the sky.

Cole scanned the dorm. The beds of the other two boys were made. He couldn't believe it. They let him sleep in.

The T-shirt and hospital pants were missing. He remembered Dale helping him take them off last night and throwing them in the corner. He searched under the bed and came up empty.

Cole walked out of the dorm area in his underwear. What else could he do? The hallway was quiet. Where was everybody? Only as he approached the nurses' station did he hear the radio at a soft volume. Cynthia was sitting by herself, flipping through a magazine. Timmy and Kenny were playing cards. He didn't see Beatrice and Laura Jean.

"Cole, for Pete's sake." Peggy came out of the nurses' station with a pile of folders.

"I couldn't find my clothes."

"Daniel picked them up for the laundry. Here, let's get you some clean stuff." She retraced her steps back to the station and tossed the files on a desk. She locked the door and approached Cole.

"There'll be a fresh pair in the supply cabinet." She fumbled with some keys and stopped. "Good heavens, you stink like a locker room. You're going to take a shower. You've got fresh jockeys and socks?"

Cole nodded, embarrassed.

"Kenny?" Peggy called. "Come here and get some shampoo and soap for Cole. He's gonna shower."

Kenny was at their sides in an instant.

"Good. You look alive again." He accepted the soaps from Peggy.

Cole turned toward the shower and saw Timmy standing nearby, watching. He was smiling shyly and rocking on his feet.

"Hey, Timmy."

"Hey, Cole." Without warning, Timmy turned and scampered back to the common room.

The shower made him feel better. Less grimy. Kenny stayed outside and talked constantly, but Cole couldn't follow. Between Kenny and the sound of running water, he started getting really drowsy again under the spray. He might've even dozed off a little, because without warning, his body thumped against the wall. It he'd been leaning toward the open space where the shower curtain should've been, he would've crashed to the floor.

Sitting at the table not long after his shower, he started getting sleepy all over again.

"So, what was it like for you?" Kenny asked.

Cole took a bite of his sandwich. He really needed to eat. He held up an index finger, chewed, and swallowed.

"I don't really remember."

Kenny sat back, frustrated. He'd never had electric shock treatment. Timmy took a bite of his sandwich, sitting quietly and clearly listening.

Cynthia was a different story. Cole had expected her to be pumping him with questions, but if anything, she seemed disinterested and a little unkempt. Even though she had the angry facial scars, her hair had always been brushed before. Now it looked straggly.

"My head feels like it's filled with cotton balls. I keep getting tired."

"That's what happened to Timmy," Kenny said. "He was real sleepy."

Timmy looked annoyed. Cole could understand. It was like someone was stealing his story or sharing his secrets.

"Did you see anything scary like yesterday?"

Cole didn't want to talk about how he had seen Timmy screaming and fighting before having his own shock treatments. That could be embarrassing for him. He'd leave that part out.

"Yeah. It was like the screaming walls again. This time, it was the walls inside that room." Cole thought about whether to go further. "And then I saw strange things last night. Maybe they were, like, nightmares."

Timmy nodded, satisfied.

"What about your demons? Are they gone now?" said Kenny.

Cole had to consider this. Something was different.

"Yeah. I mean, it's only been a day, but...maybe, yeah. I don't know." That was true, no demons that he could remember.

"What about last night?" Kenny said.

Yeah, what about last night? Cole wanted to talk about what he'd experienced, but he had been thinking about parceling them out gradually—mostly because he couldn't figure out what was real and what wasn't.

"I saw the leaper again. And her baby."

Timmy's eyes flickered. Kenny leaned forward with his elbows on the table. Even Cynthia's expression perked up a little, though she still seemed distracted and withdrawn. Cole hoped she wasn't mad at him.

"It was like I was with her the whole time."

"You mean when she threw the baby and jumped?" The first words from Cynthia.

"Before that, even. From when she ran up the stairs with the baby." Cole told them the entire tale, leaving out the part of Cynthia and Timmy lying dead on the steps instead of the girl.

"Man. That's fucking strange," Kenny whispered.

They all agreed but could go no further in their assessment because lunchtime was over.

◆

A staff member Cole hadn't seen before came in at noon.

"That's Roy," Kenny said. "He's the nurse who substitutes for Dale."

"I'm just an aide, not a nurse," Roy said to Cole. "Kenny forgets that."

Kenny shrugged and smiled.

"And you are?"

"I'm Cole."

Roy extended his hand and Cole shook it. "Nice to meet you."

"Can we go outside?" Kenny said.

"If you're all good."

After chores they all went outside, but Roy was no Dale. He didn't play anything, even though he was younger than Dale, a lot younger really, and should *want* to play. Instead, Roy just sat on the steps smoking a cigarette. It was like he was keeping a keen eye on the whole place.

In some ways, Cole was glad Roy didn't want to do anything organized. Cole's exhaustion wasn't dissipating and his mind was still foggy. He begged off Kenny's suggestion for another game of H-O-R-S-E, which Kenny didn't seem to mind. Kenny and Timmy played it by themselves.

Cole would've stuck with Cynthia, but she disappeared when they came outside. He scanned the grounds and couldn't find her. He certainly didn't want to hang out with Beatrice or Laura Jean. When he got right down to it, he was glad to be alone. There was a big oak tree with lots of shade inside the curved driveway before the main entrance. Cole headed for that and found himself a comfortable spot by the tree trunk to lean against. He thought he might fall asleep if he sat too long. He decided he didn't care, and indeed fell into a catnap within seconds.

Voices came and went as if riding on the breeze, but they remained on the very edge of his awareness. Many were adults he didn't recognize, staff or patients working outside. Every now and again Kenny laughed in response to Timmy's H-O-R-S-E shots. It was a happy sound.

The smell of cigarette smoke woke him. His vision was blurry when he opened his eyes, and he blinked them rapidly. He was momentarily confused at the unfamiliar scene. Then he remembered. Under the oak tree, and he'd taken a nap. The trunk was digging into his spine. He stretched and shifted position.

That's when he noticed someone sitting against the tree to his left. He craned his neck to peer around it.

Lambert. Relaxing and smoking.

"Hey, Lambert."

"Afternoon, young master Nightshade."

Cole smiled. "I didn't hear you come over."

"I know, son, you was out like a light. Those shock treatments will do that to you."

Cole didn't reply. He didn't have to. Lambert seemed to know what was what.

"You've been causing quite a stir, my boy."

"I have?" Cole shifted position again and sat cross-legged.

"Mm-hm. Word's out you're a seer. The haunts have been making themselves known to you."

"Yeah, well. I wish they weren't."

Lambert chuckled and took another puff. "Wishing is one thing. Reality is another."

Voices of staff and patients floated to his ears once again. Cole could clearly hear Kenny cheering on Timmy.

"I dreamt about my grandmother last night. In the dream, she said I was like a radio transmitter which has the ability to tune into these things. Not all people can do that."

"Most can't. That's what makes it a special gift. Course, you can't talk about it too loud. People'll think you're crazy. End up in a mental asylum." Lambert cracked up with his own joke.

Cole had to smile, too.

"People hear about it anyway. Your ability, I mean. The animals certainly know about it. They know you're here and they've been coming to check you out."

Cole twitched. "What about the animals?"

"Shoot, boy. Surely you've seen."

He had. The foxes, the birds, the sounds outside the window late at night. "Yeah."

"Look yonder." Lambert pointed toward the woods in the general direction of where the foxes had showed up yesterday. A herd of deer stood stock still. They were looking straight at Cole. Some patients and workers had seen the herd, too, and they were pointing at it and obviously talking about it. Others were pointing at Cole and obviously talking about him. What could they possibly be saying?

"Gives me the creeps," Cole said in a low voice.

"Well, there's nothing you can do. The animals just *know*. I think it's some kind of instinct. Animals are smarter than humans sometime. It's the people you gotta worry about."

"Do I need to worry? About the people, I mean?"

"Would it do any good?"

"I suppose not," Cole said, although Lambert hadn't answered his question. Or maybe he did.

"You just need to be alert. Be on your toes. Some folks hear you're a seer and they think you're bringing the spirits out. And some of those are angry spirits."

"Why do the other patients have to worry? They didn't do anything to the ghosts." Cole was positive this was true. It wasn't the patients' fault. "I mean, I know this asylum had some bad things happen here. My nana told me."

Lambert's gaze returned to the deer. Cole followed suit.

They seemed to be peeling away one at a time and entering the woods. Cole was grateful.

"And she's right. This has been a hellish place for some. Still is in many respects. Things'll get worse before they get better. But…" Lambert turned his head and looked directly at Cole. "It's not the patients you got to worry about."

A chill raced up and down Cole's spine. "I saw the Creeper last night. That's two nights in a row."

Now it was Lambert's turn to flinch. He took another drag of his cigarette. When it was all the way at the filter, he snuffed it out in the grass. His hands trembled.

"Tell me about what you saw last night."

Cole told him about the hands touching his back and shoulders and being flipped over. Then there was the face. "If Kenny didn't turn over, I don't know what would've happened."

Lambert rubbed his face with his left hand. Cole could feel his fear. It was like heat radiating off of a bonfire. "The Creeper is hard to get a handle on. I'm sure you heard the stories. You know, that it hunts down children and feeds on them. I'm not saying that's not true. But for the longest time I thought the Creeper was something inside a child. Something that eats away the boy or girl from within themselves. It's planted there by parents or mean-spirited adults."

Cole was baffled. "You mean it's not a real monster?"

Lambert scrunched his whole face and looked up at the mountain peaks in the distance. "Son, here's where I can't explain it. Many kids get hurt by their own anger or sadness. As I said, adults plant it."

"So, the Creeper is part of them."

Lambert hesitated. "Yes."

"But…"

Cole waited for him to continue.

"Sometimes, there's something more than what's inside. Something outside gains a power that can infect people and turn them into the Creeper. I believe that force is in this asylum. Not everyone who works here is bad. There's some fine people. But some are drawn here, and they take on that force. That *evil* force.

"It doesn't come alive all the time. For a while it can hibernate like bears do in the winter. But now I think someone has become the Creeper."

"Wait. Now you're saying it's real?"

"Yes, son. And I don't know who or what it is."

"Does it really eat kids?

Lambert looked at Cole for the longest time. Cole wondered if he had forgotten the question. Finally, the old man answered.

"Yes. And you're describing him. Those rags you said were hanging from him? Those aren't made of cloth. That's the leftover skin of vanished children."

"Oh. Shit." Cole barely mouthed the words.

They sat in silence for a bit, and then Lambert seemed to be getting ready to say something. Cole broke the silence first. He needed to know.

"Kenny said that the Creeper doesn't let you see it and live." The last part Cole whispered.

"Kenny said that? I don't think that's true."

Cole could tell that Lambert was lying. He should know you couldn't fool a fellow seer.

"I first heard about the Creeper many years ago. Twenty, maybe? Anyhow, the story's been around. Maybe for as long as this building's been open. People talk about it. Like, how he looks. If everyone who sees it gets killed, how do the stories get passed on? Did you ever think of that?"

Cole considered this. It certainly made sense. He felt a little relieved.

"Still," said Lambert, "you've gotta be careful. Never be alone."

"Yeah, okay."

"I mean that, Cole. Never be by yourself. If it's a night and you see that thing, you scream bloody murder. You wake everyone up. You make sure that nurse comes running."

Kenny and Timmy crossed the driveway and headed in their direction. Kenny had the basketball and dribbled it in the pavement. When he reached the grass, the bounce wasn't good and he missed the ball. He tripped over it instead. Kenny got up, laughing his head off, and grabbed it. Even Timmy giggled at the sight. Cole had to smile too. Both boys jogged over to the tree.

"Sleeping beauty." Kenny gave Cole a playful kick in the knee.

Timmy was puzzled. "Shouldn't he get a kiss then?"

"No, Timms, I ain't kissing him, just teasing him. Hey Lambert." Kenny plopped to the ground. Timmy followed, but not before surveying for the best spot and descending slowly.

"Did you win, Kenny?" Lambert said.

"Nah. Timmy kicked my ass. As usual."

Timmy grinned while focusing on a small acorn in the grass.

"The young man is grace under pressure." Kenny added. Timmy's face blushed to a mild pink, but he looked delighted.

Kenny lay down and spread out on the grass with his hands folded behind his head. The oak leaves above rustled in the breeze. Shadows passed over Kenny's face.

"So, Lambert. Is Cole's brain back to normal?"

Cole groaned. "I'm right here, you know."

Lambert hummed under his breath and didn't reply right away. Kenny lifted his head up to look directly at the old man.

"Oh, he's gettin' there," Lambert said. "He's been talking to the angels."

Cole shifted his head to look at Kenny, who shrugged in reply. Who were the angels? Were these the haunts and spirits Lambert was talking about?

"I've been talking to Lambert about the Creeper." Cole felt he needed to say something.

Kenny abruptly sat up while Timmy dropped the acorn he was playing with. It landed in front of his shin, forgotten.

"What about it?"

"It appeared by my bed last night and touched me. The thing actually flipped me over so I could see its face."

The only sounds were Lambert's humming and the leaves being tossed in the wind. Puffy, fair-weather clouds raced toward the mountains. Their shadows seemed to be skipping toward the peaks.

Timmy leaned into Kenny. "Cole's still here, so the Creeper didn't kill him."

"Maybe it's not the Creeper," said Kenny.

"I know what I saw. Two times now. Skin of dead kids was hanging off it." Cole went on to describe the details. For good measure, he added the part with Nana.

Neither Timmy nor Kenny could contribute any new observations. Other than a few questions, the other two boys quieted, and everyone seemed to consider the latest reports privately. Cole was actually a little concerned about Lambert, who was still making humming sounds.

Out of the blue, Timmy said, "Where's Cynthia?"

Kenny looked sheepish, which was unusual. "I'm pretty sure she had to go with Mr. Plovac."

"That's bad," said Timmy, rotating his head to examine the grounds.

"I saw her go over by the woods," Kenny said. "Shit. The bastard."

"Who's that?" Cole said.

"Plovac's an aide for the men's unit. He used to be on the women's unit, but they transferred him," Kenny replied.

"What's that got to do with Cynthia?"

Kenny glowered at Cole, who felt uncomfortable under the glare. He'd hate to see how Kenny looked if he was really mad.

"Plovac gives her candy, which she'll share with us later. But in return, she has to give him a hand job or a blow job." Kenny spit off to the side. "She was getting kinda moody this morning. She told me what was up."

Cole felt devastated. "God. Does this happen a lot?"

"Whenever the fucker's in the mood." Kenny spat again.

"Why doesn't anybody stop him?"

"Because this is Saint Edwards. This is how it's run," Lambert said. "The damn, shameful things adults do to children."

"I know," Cole said. This got everyone's attention.

"What? What'd do you mean?" Kenny's expression had eased. He seemed like he had softened.

"My foster mother. She did it to me." The memory of Dorie getting into bed with him raced through his mind.

"Wait. Wait. Your foster mother went all the way? With you? Had sex with you?"

"What did I just say?" Cole's fists were clenched.

Beside him, Lambert mumbled and shook his head. Timmy's mouth hung open in bewilderment.

"But you're just a little kid. Losing your cherry at eleven," Kenny said.

Cole couldn't figure out if Kenny was impressed or jealous. "I was almost twelve."

"Man, I thought I was young."

Cole waited for Kenny to tell the rest. When he didn't, Cole prompted him. "Well, how old were you?"

"Fourteen. She was my teacher."

"Your teacher?" Lambert said. Cole felt his disgust. It was like the old man was exhaling it into the air.

"Yeah, my English teacher."

Lambert muttered again, "The damn, shameful things adults do it children."

"Nobody said anything? The school wasn't mad?" Cole said.

"They never found out."

"Really?" Cole said. "How come?"

"Because I killed her."

Kenny's reply was nonchalant. Cole wasn't sure if he'd heard him right.

"Felt like the right thing to do." Kenny said.

Cole collapsed back into the trunk of the tree. His head was spinning again. He couldn't tell if this was the result of his conversations with Lambert and Kenny or the aftereffects of the shock treatments. It could be either or both.

God, he didn't know. His mind was still fuzzy around the edges.

Timmy hopped up and called, "Cynthia." He took off in a loping run.

Cole craned his neck and saw the girl slowly approaching. Kenny also got to his feet.

"Damn, she doesn't look good."

Cole had to agree. She looked pale and shaky. Her steps were slow and disjointed like she was drunk. He'd seen his foster parents in that condition a couple of times.

"She cut her own face up last year," Kenny said.

"No way." Cole couldn't believe it. People didn't *do* that.

"Yeah, she did. She tried to explain it once. Said it made her feel better. The pain kinda took the bad feelings away."

Cole's heart felt like it was going to beat through his ribs. "Bad feelings from what?" Deep inside, though, Cole had an awful feeling he knew exactly what.

Kenny looked straight ahead. "Her uncle or grandfather or some such messed around with her since she was little. Got away with it, too."

Cole's entire chest ached for her. "Jeez."

Kenny nodded. "That fucker Plovac must have second sight. He pounced on her right away. Just like a lion does when it sees a wounded gazelle."

Beside him, Cole heard Lambert mutter, "The damn things adults do to kids."

Timmy came to an immediate stop just before plowing into Cynthia. He said something softly. She gave the tiniest shake of the head. Timmy cautiously raised a hand to push back an errant lock of hair. The gesture was gentle, and Cynthia nodded thanks.

The two continued over to the tree. Cole stood and stepped by Kenny. When Cynthia and Timmy reached them, Cynthia held out a paper bag to Kenny.

"Jelly beans, I think."

Kenny's arm raised in fits and starts. He seemed unsure

what to do, but finally accepted the bag. "You don't have to do this, you know."

"Who's gonna put a stop to it? No one would believe me. Besides, I can handle it. He could do worse."

"I'm sorry, young lady." Lambert struggled to stand and braced against the tree to keep from falling. Cole and Kenny assisted in guiding him upright.

"Thanks, Lambert."

"Look, here he comes," said Timmy.

Cole and Kenny spun around, but Cynthia kept her back to the direction Timmy was pointing.

"Which one is he?"

"That big fucker," Kenny said. "With the oily hair."

Cole spotted him. The white uniform wrapping his frame made Plovac stand out like a beacon. The muscles on his upper body flexed under his tight-fitting shirt. Violence rippled off the man with each step.

"Can we beat him in?" Cynthia said.

"Yeah," Kenny said. "If we move now. Let's go."

Cynthia spun and strode toward the building. Kenny and Timmy flanked her like bodyguards. After a few feet, Kenny called over his shoulder to Cole.

"Hang back and see if he does anything."

Cole said okay although he wasn't sure what he'd be looking for. Lambert placed a hand on his shoulder, and they strolled in the general direction of the front steps.

"You grew up in the mountains."

"Yessir," Cole said.

"So you know about the outdoors and such."

Cole nodded and kept watch on Plovac. As the man got closer, he looked even meaner. His eyes glinted like a reflection off a gun.

"I could sure use some help working on the plantings and the flowers out here. Do you know enough to lend a hand?"

Cole realized what Lambert was doing. He was making small talk so as not to make them look suspicious as they watched Plovac. "Sure, I can do that." He meant it, too. Being outside would be a way to spend his time and break up the monotony. "Do you really mean it?" This last question he sort of whispered.

Lambert chuckled. "Of course, son. I ain't making nothing up."

As they approached the main steps, Cole faltered slightly. He glanced up, expecting the baby and girl to be rushing to their deaths.

"No leapers today," Lambert said gently.

Thank God. Cole checked on Plovac's location.

He was a mere ten feet away. Their eyes met. Cole couldn't pull his away. Plovac appeared to relish the connection. He smirked.

"What're you lookin' at, you little freak?"

Cole opened his mouth but no words came out.

"That's what I thought. Don't let me catch you anywhere near me. Got it?" Plovac didn't wait for a reply. He stomped up the stairs, brushing past Roy, their nurses' aide for the day.

Lambert's hand was still on Cole's shoulder. He squeezed it once. "See? People know who you are. I think he's afraid of you."

That wasn't what Cole expected to hear. "Sure didn't sound like it."

All the while, Cole watched Plovac enter the building. He

noticed that Roy did, too. Only when Plovac was out of sight did Roy turn back.

"Okay, Cole. Let's go inside." He nodded to Lambert.

Cole sensed Lambert returning the nod.

"We'll talk more, Cole."

11

Chaz Tells the Sad Stories

EVIE CORRALLED THE GROUP INTO the hallway while Chaz
shut the entrance to the women's ward. As he scooted around
everyone quieted.

"We can't go to the fourth floor, but I do want to talk
about what happened there. If we were upstairs and walked
down the hall that way"—Chaz pointed to his left—"we'd
come to a small alcove. I'm not sure what it was for. It's not
very big. Large enough for a sitting chair and end table with
a lamp, but that's about it. There's been speculation that
maybe it was a waiting area for the doctors or other big muck-
ety-mucks who had their offices on the floor."

Chaz fell silent in preparation for the next barrage of information. The group perceptively leaned into the verbal gap.

"There's also a decent-sized window with a nice view of
the front grounds. Actually, it's a double-hung window with
wooden grilles in a colonial style. I had to google that so I
could describe it like I knew what I was talking about."

The adults smiled. The kids were getting a little restless, so he'd need to move along.

"There have been at least two suicides from that window."

A couple of mouth-shaped *O*s but no gasps.

"One for sure occurred in the nineteen fifties. There's a record of it. Believe it or not, it was a nurse. The talk was that she'd been dumped, probably by one of the doctors or an asylum official. She lost it. Ran screaming to the alcove area above and threw herself out the window."

"That's not easy to do," said the dad. His kids turned and looked at him.

"That's what I understand," said Chaz. "Although I've never tried it, either. They make it look so easy on TV."

"Did they ever find out who her lover was?" one of the college girls said.

"No. Well, at least *we* haven't. But we keep checking."

The oldest kid said, "Does she haunt the place?"

"Ah. Good question. No one has actually seen her—as far as we know. However, there have been many reports of screaming and sounds of running. Both here on the third floor and on the fourth floor. There's been speculation that it's her. The fact that the sounds are on both floors got us thinking that maybe she got dumped here and then ran up the stairs. That's just guesswork. But the sounds have been heard by many people."

"What about the other suicide?" said the Beard.

"That one's a lot more ghastly. And we don't know much about it. There are two accounts, and both go way back. One version says that a teenage girl showed up with a baby when this place was the boys' school. She demanded to see a particular boy. Evidently she claimed that he was the father. The boy was sent for, and when he arrived at the main office, he either denied knowing the girl or denied the baby was his.

"The headmaster was at a loss. What should he do with the distraught young lady who was toting around this baby? While he was enlisting help from staff, the girl wandered off and either climbed to the fourth-floor alcove or somehow got on the roof."

Chaz paused again to let the suspense build.

"The outcome was the same either way. The girl tossed the baby through the window or off the roof and she jumped after it."

A familiar pattern of distressed vocalizations spilled from many in the group. The story was desperately sad. Chaz didn't want the mood to linger too long, so he pushed ahead with his narrative. "The second version is essentially the same, except it was a nurse who was in the same predicament and it happened in the early days of Saint Edwards. This time, instead of a selfish teenage boy, the culprit was one of the psychiatrists."

The two college girls exchanged whispered comments. The wives also conferred among themselves. The men stood around awkwardly. Chaz jumped ahead to what he considered the most interesting part.

"The girl and the baby have also been known to haunt Saint Edwards. But for whatever reason, only a handful of patients have seen her. The accounts are similar and have spread out over decades.

"They appear to someone outside in broad daylight. There's a scream from above, the patient looks up and sees something falling. As it gets closer, the patient realizes it's a baby. It splatters on the front steps of the building. Shortly thereafter, the mother is seen diving from her position with the same terrible outcome."

Evie took over. "As you can imagine, the patients who reported seeing these images were forever troubled by them. You can't unsee them." She held the group's gaze. "Shall we move on to the second floor and the pediatric ward?"

Wham. Superb timing on Evie's part.

12

Kenny and the Milk Truck

September 1962

"HEY THERE, KENNY. HOW'RE Y'ALL this evening? It's certainly more comfortable with the humidity down. Those storms just wrung the moisture out of the sky. But you youngsters probably don't mind it. My, my. Who's that with you?"

A big colored lady swooped down as Kenny led Cole into the surprisingly large kitchen. The lady wore cat's-eye glasses and had a huge smile that showed the brightest teeth Cole had ever seen.

Kenny performed an exaggerated bow at the waist and extended his arm out to Cole. "Evening, Miss Augusta. May I present to you our newest resident, Cole Nightshade."

Cole found himself speechless at Kenny's theatrical introduction.

"Cole Nightshade. Well, well, well. Mister Lambert told us all about you. I'm so pleased to finally meet you." Miss Augusta dried her meaty hands on a pristine apron and thrust her hand in his direction.

"Um, hi." Cole shook the offered hand. In the blink of an eye, the woman clasped her hands on both of Cole's shoulders.

"Let me look at you." She did, too. Face, shoulders, and chest as if looking for damage. "Lambert was right. A big strong boy. Just like our Kenny." She let go, and Cole had the sensation of dropping a half inch to reach the ground. He felt a proud swelling in his chest, being compared to Kenny. Cole snuck a glance at the older boy and received a thumbs-up gesture.

"You're a seer, just like Lambert. My goodness." Miss Augusta leaned closer to Cole. Her face was covered with a thin sheen of perspiration. She smelled like the caramelized sugar Nana used to make. "There are many, and I mean *many*, poor souls here," she whispered. "Don't fear them, child. They're just lost. Lonely. They eventually leave. Some do, anyway. They find their way out. I know there are some I haven't seen in the longest time."

"You're a seer?"

"I tend to see the ladies. And the children. The children are sometimes confused. They need consoling."

"Does that make you sad?" Cole asked. "Seeing ghost kids, I mean."

Miss Augusta nodded. "Oh, yes, honey. They need someone to say that things'll be all right."

Kenny stood back and looked around. He'd probably heard this kind of talk before if he regularly came down to pick up the meals. Metal pans clanged against one another as other staff doled out food into containers or washed the containers once they were emptied.

"But enough of this," Miss Augusta said. She stepped back and reached for a metal cart piled with flat containers of various sizes covered in aluminum foil. "You're all set to go. Kenny knows the routine. What you need to do now is call for Daniel, who'll take you in the elevator. You drop the women's containers off first, and then you go to your ward. You'll leave the empty containers, any leftovers, and the cart outside the ward door around seven. Got that?"

"Yes, ma'am. I got that."

"Good, child." She patted his head. "We'll be seeing you in the future, I hope."

"Yes, ma'am. I hope so, too."

Kenny and Cole left the kitchen with the cart. "There's an elevator?" Cole asked.

"Yeah, but there's a key, and Daniel and the doctors are the only ones who can use it. It's down near where Daniel keeps his little maintenance office."

Daniel was easy to find, just down the hall and cleaning out a broom closet from the looks of it.

"Boys," he called as they approached with their clanging cart.

"We're here for our ride," Kenny announced.

"Right-o. Let's get the keys." Daniel rummaged around the office and picked up a set off a pegboard, took two steps, and halted. "Oops, wrong ones." He traced his steps back and exchanged the set in his hand for another. "I should label these more clearly."

"What was the first set for?" Kenny asked.

"Oh, those. The tunnel." Daniel motioned in the direction of a dark doorway with a locked collapsible gate.

"Hey, what is that? I saw it yesterday." Cole said.

"That's right. I guess you would've. That, young man, is the Dead Tunnel."

Cole hadn't anticipated a name like that. He shuddered, and Daniel chuckled in reply.

"It does sound sorta spooky, don't it? But it's not, really. When they renovated the building from a school to a sanitarium, they added this tunnel so they could wheel out bodies for burial without being seen by the other patients. They didn't want to upset them. After all, people did die here. Still do."

Cole couldn't imagine trying to sneak a dead body down this tunnel. "Do they still use it?"

Daniel stepped back into his office for the keys he'd just returned. "Not for that. Nowadays the county coroner will come and pick up a body out by the loading dock in the back. People don't go through here much anymore—except for maybe certain kind of deliveries. Also, I think it serves as a fallout shelter. Here let me show you."

"Cool," Kenny said.

"Have you ever seen it?" Cole asked him.

"Uh-uh. This is our lucky day."

Daniel fumbled with the lock. It opened with a noisy click, and the handyman collapsed the gate with a pull.

Cole had thought the blackness behind the gate was the interior of the tunnel. Instead there was a pitch black door—a solid metal one by the sound of the lock and the effort it took Daniel to swing the door inward. The hinges groaned as if it hadn't been opened for a long time.

The boys looked past Daniel to spy into the tunnel. The interior was unlit. Cole imagined a creature ready to pounce on them from the darkness. Or—and this thought made Cole lean backwards—the Creeper.

Daniel patted beyond the interior doorframe. "Ah, here it

is." A light switch clicked and a trail of florescent tube lights illuminated. The lights went on forever.

"How far does it go?" Kenny asked.

"About fifty yards. Maybe a little more. There's a slight curve, so you can't see the end from here. It's actually built into the side of a hill so you don't notice it from the outside. There's just an opening at the end. Like a cave or a big drain with a driveway in front."

Cole peered down the tunnel. The flatness of the floor would accommodate a gurney that could wheel a dead body. There was an indentation in the wall farther down on the left. With a little more searching, Cole saw another on the right.

"What are those? They look like doorways."

Daniel followed where Cole was pointing. "Oh, storage rooms. Tools and things in the room on the left. On the right was kind of a makeshift morgue if they needed it. Sometimes the grave wouldn't be ready for the burial or the weather wouldn't permit transport. They had to put the body somewhere. There's even a refrigeration unit. Not sure if works anymore, though."

"Man, that's sick," Cole said.

"Really? I think it's cool." Kenny looked fascinated by the whole thing.

Daniel snorted at their reactions. "Okay, you guys. Your dinner's getting cold. Let's get upstairs before Nurse Stern gets on her high horse."

The stop at the women's ward was pretty depressing. Cole was expecting to walk into a room full of women who'd make a big deal over them, sort of like moms would do. Instead the patients on the floor were just plain sad. A couple of women stood or sat frozen in place, sort of like Laura Jean, who often curled up in a fetal position. Others would sit and stare outside or thumb through a magazine mindlessly; the only sounds they made were heartbreaking sighs. One of them was Mrs. D, who'd warmly greeted him and Kenny when she brought the lunch on his second day. Then there was a lady who came running up to them, shouting, "I won't let you touch my food. You can't do it." Two staffers were needed to drive her away. Finally there was another lady, about forty years old, who was wearing a little girl dress, sort of like Shirley Temple. She even had a big bow in her hair. A lot of her legs were showing; they were wrinkled and hairy.

"What was with the one lady with the dress?" Cole said.

Kenny knew exactly who he meant. "I don't know, man. She was creepy. I wonder if they tried giving shocks to her."

Daniel escorted them to the elevator to bring them down a floor to the kids' ward. A scream, followed by cries of "No! No!" shattered the silence in the hallway.

Cole jumped, and he pivoted in the direction of the other two.

But Kenny and Daniel showed no indication that they'd heard it. They didn't flinch or spin around. They walked along like nothing was happening.

Cole was hearing this on his own.

He turned his head and caught sight of a nurse tearing away from the door to the women's ward. She ran down the hall toward them, looking behind her as if someone, or *something*, was in hot pursuit. The nurse reached the stairs and tried to take two at a time, but her foot caught the lip of a stair. She crashed forward, saving her face from smashing into an edge by extending a hand in the nick of time—and dislocating her thumb. She yelped in pain.

The nurse spun her head again, and her eyes and mouth sprung open in terror. She scrambled to her feet. Both knees were bleeding behind torn white hose. Pulling on the handrail, she leapt and clawed her way to the fourth floor and disappeared out of view.

"Hey, man?" Kenny and Daniel were at the elevator. "You coming?"

"Uh, yeah. Sorry." Cole scurried to join them in the elevator.

Minutes later, as he and Kenny helped unpack the dinner, Cole was able to quell his shakes.

The actual dinner was a somber affair. Cynthia sat listlessly and barely picked at her meal. Cole worried that she might be turning into those unmoving women he'd just seen in the ward above. He couldn't imagine what it was like to sit completely still like a statue all day, every day. He'd go crazy with boredom.

The bag of jelly beans that Cynthia had received from the aide for her favors sat on the counter by the trays that had contained their dinner. Cole wondered if they shouldn't just throw it out.

"I thought of that," Kenny told him earlier on the way to the kitchen. "I tried it before, but she gets madder if we toss them. It's weird. The best thing to do is have some and let her see us have some. Then we can throw it out—or give them all to Beatrice. That's what Timmy and me have done before. Laura Jean doesn't eat them."

So they each had a handful after dinner but didn't make a big deal of it. The candy was stale and tasted like crap. Even Beatrice didn't want any more after a few bites. They dumped the remainder in the garbage. Cynthia didn't comment one way or the other.

乄

Later, after showers and lights out, Cole stretched out in bed on top of the sheets. He was feeling almost back to normal, although his brain still seemed a little groggy at times. One thing kept running through his mind from earlier in the day.

Because I killed her.

Kenny killed someone. He mentioned it so matter-of-factly that it had to be true. Cole had never met someone who was a murderer. He didn't know what to think about it. Was that why Kenny was in here? What would adults do to a kid who killed a teacher? And why did Kenny do it? Wouldn't he have liked what she did with him?

The last thought caught him short.

Maybe he didn't. How had Cole felt about what Dorie did to him?

Well, it was complicated. He understood that. But did you kill somebody over it? Cole could see for the first time how maybe somebody could. Adults were supposed to take care of kids, not take advantage of them.

In the next bed, Kenny was silent. Cole knew he was still awake. After just a couple of days he could now identify when Kenny, or Timmy for that matter, was asleep based on his breathing.

"Kenny?" Cole whispered.

"Yeah?"

Cole thought for a second and plowed ahead with his question. "How many people have you killed?"

Silence from the next bed.

Cole heard a few crickets outside. The nocturnal animals were quieter than they had been. The breeze filtering through the trees was a little cooler than previous nights.

Cole wondered if maybe he'd made Kenny mad.

"Three." Unemotional and to the point.

"Oh."

Now what was he supposed to say?

"Why?"

Again, Kenny was silent for a short while.

"I'll tell you about them sometime. Not now, though."

"That's okay."

Cole sunk a little more into his bed. The quiet was peaceful, but there was an edge to the air around the asylum. Maybe having Roy here in the evening when he had gotten used to Dale had something to do with it. He wasn't sure.

The images of the nurse running and screaming? That could be it too. Or the creepy women's ward.

"Cole?"

Cole started. "Yeah?"

"One of them was my father."

Cole sat up and shifted to the edge of the bed. Planted his feet on the floor. The moonlight was bright enough for him to see Kenny lying on his back on top of the cover sheet like Cole had been. His hands were clasped behind his head. He stared at the ceiling.

"You killed your father?" Cole whispered.

"Yeah. My old man was a jerk. I mean, a real first-class asshole. He and my uncle had a still up the mountain from our home. It was way back and evidently in the family for years. He'd bring his moonshine home. Him and Mom would drink it. Mom passed out usually, or just sat around when she drunk the stuff. She wasn't good for nothing when she was shitfaced. But that was better than my old man. He'd get mean. He'd beat the crap out of me and sometimes Mom for the littlest shit. This was, like, all the time.

"He held down his job despite being a shitfaced drunk. He was a milkman. He'd deliver milk all over the county, going up the mountains and down into the hollers. He'd take me to help when he was too hungover. Sometimes he even let me drive the truck.

"I'd been on his route a lot, and I knew the spot where I'd try it. I just needed the nerve. There's a section of switchback roads over by Catawba. I knew a spot with a drop-off. A big fucking drop-off right along a big curve."

Kenny paused and yawned softly. Cole gripped the edge of the bed with both hands, waiting. Finally, Kenny was ready.

"This one morning in the winter it was still dark. And he sure wasn't sober. He was sleeping on the floor of the truck and I was driving. We never saw traffic on that road that early, and this day was no different. Right before we got to the curve with the drop off, I rigged the gas pedal with a piece of wood. I had it measured and everything. My old man didn't even notice when I was setting it up. He kinda mumbled, but that's about it.

"I drove for a straightaway section, just steering. The truck kept accelerating. Right before the curve, I opened the door and just hopped out. It hurt like shit. I rolled more than I thought I would.

"After I stopped, I climbed down to look for where the truck went over the cliff. It took a while to find it. The truck must've gone end over end all the way down the mountainside. It was trashed. The milk bottles were in pieces. My old man was cut nearly in half."

Kenny unclasped his hands and stretched briefly. He crossed his arms over his chest like a shield, each hand rubbing the opposite shoulder.

"I wasn't too far from home, so I hauled ass to make it

back before Mom got up. She was bombed the night before, so I knew I had some time. Plus, it was Christmas vacation and I didn't have to worry about being late for school. I snuck in and got in bed hours before the cops came to tell us about the accident."

Cole remained on the edge of the bed. Kenny didn't seem upset. He could have been talking about doing chores or a day at school. Still, Cole felt terrible for him. How could a person treat their kid like this?

"I'm sorry, Kenny."

"Thanks. But don't be. He was a dirtbag. There's lots I haven't told you about him. Someday, maybe I will."

Cole nodded, although he couldn't tell if Kenny saw.

"Are you and Nurse Peggy, you know, doing it?"

Kenny chuckled. "You're full of surprises tonight." His head turned to Cole. "Yeah. We hit it off right away. If she's in the mood, she wakes me up early morning. Brings me a rubber. It doesn't happen all the time."

"Isn't she like an adult, though?" Cole couldn't help thinking of Kenny's English teacher.

"Sorta, but not really. She's only twenty-one or something. I'm almost seventeen. Close enough.

This was a lot to ponder. Cole eased back into bed.

"I got a question for you," Kenny said.

"Okay."

"Any more demons?"

Cole folded his arms over his chest. He had to think about this.

"Since the shock therapy?" He sat up again. "No."

"You're seeing ghosts, though, right?"

"Yeah. I think."

"So, it's like I said. There's no demons. They're in your head. But the ghosts are real."

Cole reflected on this. "Wait, how can the ghosts be real, but the demons not?"

"Because, kiddo, the demons are you." Kenny turned his handsome face directly to Cole. "You're scared of yourself or something. You do that stupid counting to keep from being yourself. You gotta let yourself go, man."

Cole slid to a prone position for the second time within a minute. It made no sense, but somehow sounded true. How the hell would Kenny know this? He rubbed his temples as if the pressure would make him understand.

You're scared of yourself.

What does that mean?

Never mind that. What does "let myself go" mean?

"Goodnight, Cole."

With seconds, Kenny's breathing *did* change. The older boy had fallen asleep like he didn't have a single problem in the world.

Cole was envious of that.

13

What the Creeper Did

September 1962

"GET UP, GENTLEMEN. STAND BY your beds." Nurse Stern marched into the dorm area like an army general. "Up, Cole. Now."

Cole had been in a deep, dreamless sleep. The grayness of the morning light surprised him. All the other mornings since his arrival had been sunny.

Cole stood and shook his limbs. Nurse Stern gave barely a passing glance at his sheets.

"Make your bed, grab your clothes, get dressed, and go wash up." Her tone was perfunctory.

Cole shrugged and started making his bed but risked a sideways glimpse at Kenny. Nurse Stern was paying closer attention to his sheets but still wasn't conducting her usual thorough inspection. Kenny, on the other hand, scrunched up his forehead as he watched, clearly perplexed.

Nurse Stern was alone. Normally she'd be with the

morning person—that was generally Peggy. Maybe Kenny was puzzled by her absence.

"Make your bed and get ready." Kenny had passed the stained-sheet test.

Timmy wasn't so lucky. He had been trying to make his bed before Nurse Stern approached him. As he glanced up, he looked guilty. He was even trying to pull up the top sheet.

Nurse Stern grabbed the sheet out of Timmy's hands and threw it over the end of the bed. From his position by his own bed, Cole could see a wet spot.

"Oh, man. Crap," Kenny said under his breath.

Nurse Stern growled at Timmy, who took a step backward and bumped into his night table. A crumbled tissue fell to the floor.

"Shame, Timmy. After all we've done for you. Get ready for breakfast."

Nurse Stern turned on her heels and stormed from the dorm. Cole shook slightly while Kenny's mouth hung open. Timmy whined a little and swallowed.

"Well, Timms, you might've gotten away with it this time." Kenny led the way into the bathroom.

After breakfast, a pale woman wearing a weird pink outfit swooped into the ward. In one hand she carried a book bag, which she plopped on the center dining room table. She dug out books and papers in a flash.

"A teacher?" Cole mouthed to Kenny.

Kenny shut his eyes and nodded. "Yeah, she shows up every couple of days."

The teacher, her name was Miss Harrison, reminded Cole of a rabbit. Her long, limp hair was pulled back to make two ponytails. They looked like floppy ears. She had a tendency to wrinkle her nose a lot like she was sniffing, and she sort of hopped from table to table.

Miss Harrison made sure the kids were spread out among the tables in the dining area so they didn't start messing around with each other. Then she handed out a bunch of worksheets. Cole must've completed three of those stupid things in the hour the teacher was there, and he wasn't even a fast worksheet completer. The math was pretty easy, but the English was a pain. Cole couldn't tell how many the other kids finished. He did notice that Beatrice didn't do anything other than color.

Right before lunch, Miss Harrison again opened her bag and took out piles of paperback books. She wanted them all to pick one and read it before she returned in a few days.

Everyone halfheartedly approached the pile and listlessly thumbed through the options.

Cole had never really read an entire book, so didn't know what to look for. The description on the back cover of one book about orphaned kids who lived in a boxcar stood out. He chose it and brought it back to his side table in the dorm room.

With the teacher gone, the ladies from the floor above brought their lunches. Like everyone else, they were subdued. Their mood fit the weather. The gray skies had given way to off-and-on showers. Though it was still warm, the gloomy clouds had a winter feel to them. Eating lunch helped his mood a little as Kenny talked about all the tricks he used to do to skip school. Cole thought some were funny, although he would never skip because his nana would be disappointed in him. Timmy was quiet, even by Timmy standards. He didn't look as if he was paying attention to Kenny. Cynthia was lethargic during the whole meal, moving only to eat. She had only taken three or four bites out of her sandwich.

Cole was worried about her.

Roy was back at noon, which meant that Dale was off for another day. Nurse Stern hung around through lunch to be with Roy but disappeared after everything was cleaned and put away. Throughout the morning, Nurse Stern had seemed a little frazzled. It wasn't like she made mistakes or forgot how to do things; it was more the way her face looked. The wrinkles in her forehead and eyes were more pronounced, as if she'd been concentrating too hard. And the tiniest wisp of hair had fallen from beneath her nurse cap and curled in front of her ear.

After lunch, Kenny seemed to catch everybody else's mood and sunk into the couch in the common room, looking at his book sullenly. Timmy was in a trance of sorts, and Cynthia retreated to her room. Beatrice made fewer of her noises than usual. Cole sought permission from Roy to go into the dorm.

The Boxcar Children turned out to be decent. Cole was stunned to find that he actually enjoyed reading and kept turning the pages to find out what was going to happen to the kids. He'd read almost seventy pages when he started to feel tired. Lounging on his bed with a pillow propping up his head, he marked his place in the book and set it aside. The gentle tap of raindrops on the windows was just barely perceptible. Sleep came quickly.

His chest heaved with panic. He needed to seek shelter. The obvious place was the women's ward on the third floor. There'd be help once he unlocked the door. At least another staff person...and a telephone.

The bit of the key snagged on a pocket seam and jingled across the floor several yards before the ward access door.

Picking it up, he saw he was wearing white squeaky shoes and white stockings—a nurse's uniform.

What the hell?

There was no time to figure it out now. He just needed to grab the keys and get moving.

He scooped them up and took off. Just as he reached to insert the pin and bit into the keyhole, the ward door burst open. He stumbled and caught himself before he fell through the doorframe.

The eyes of the creature staring back at him were from beyond the far reaches of evil. There was no glimmer of a soul, only inhuman darkness. The torn skin of others unfolded over its own face while shawl-like remnants draped over muscular shoulders.

"No! No!" His screams felt hollow and foreign in his ears.

He twisted away from the door and scrambled toward the stairs. Running was difficult, as he was unfamiliar with the shoes and he felt like his ankles were twisting from side to side. The lip of the first step caught the toe of his shoe. He crashed painfully to the stairs. Pushing with his hand, he noticed that his thumb was bent at a strange angle. He whimpered at the sight, then clambered to his feet when he heard the approach of the monster. His knees ached, but he still kept climbing, taking the stairs two at a time when he could.

A keening sob burst from his mouth as he entered the fourth-floor landing. His heartbeat pounded in his ears along with something else—the growling wails of the approaching figure.

The Creeper in pursuit. A thing that was supposed to be just a story, nothing real. How...how could this be?

The fourth floor had no place to hide. It was after hours

and the evening was getting late. All office doors were closed. He tried one or two but they were locked as expected.

Running down the corridor, he found a small alcove. He turned to find a small sitting area with windows overlooking the front of the asylum. This wouldn't work. There was no place to hide.

The Creeper rammed into his back. He felt like the force was shattering his spine at his waist as it pushed him toward the windows. He managed to get one hand on a window frame as his body bashed through the glass. In one final glimpse of detail, he watched as a fingernail scraped a deep slice out of the oak frame.

Then he was falling and only had the briefest view of the ledge on which his head burst.

♌

"Hey, man, there you are." Kenny practically skipped into the boys' dorm.

Cole sat up in his bed and rubbed his face. He was still shaken from the memory, even though the details were growing fuzzy.

"Sun's out," Kenny said as he plopped on his own bed. "Roy said we can go outside. You game?"

Still groggy, Cole really wasn't, but he figured it might help get his mind off the stupid nightmare. "Yeah, sure."

"Well, don't get too excited."

"Sorry, I fell asleep and had a weird dream."

"Ooh, poor baby." Kenny actually caressed Cole's face in his hands for a second.

"Stop it, man."

"C'mon, let's go. We probably don't have too much time." Kenny sprung to his feet. "We may get our pictures taken. Apparently, there's some writer doing a story about the asylum for a magazine."

Cole thought that was cool, so he jumped out of bed and followed Kenny out the door.

The girls were being pains. They thought it was too wet outside and wanted to stay in. Nurse Stern agreed to babysit them while Roy took the boys outside.

Timmy carried a football under his arm and led the way to the large green space on the grounds. Unlike Dale, who would play with them for the entire time, Roy threw the ball with them for a little while and then begged off. He seemed more interested in inspecting the grounds. For what, Cole wasn't sure, but then again he didn't care. It felt great to be moving around. And it did ease the unsettling feeling left over from his dream.

The three of them took turns playing quarterback and passing the football to an intended receiver. The third guy tried to defend against the pass. By far, Cole was the weakest passer and defender. His receiving skills weren't that terrific either. Being the oldest, Kenny could throw the longest. By far, though, the most graceful receiver was Timmy. That kid was like Spider-Man. He could leap and catch anything in his vicinity. And he was never awkward or hesitant. Kenny raved about Timmy's efforts as if he was a TV announcer.

The girls were right about things being wet, though. It didn't take long for their pajama pants to become soaked from about the knees down. It was also getting hotter with the sun out, and both Kenny and Cole stripped off their T-shirts and tucked them in the back waistband of their pants. Timmy commented that it looked like they had tails.

After a while, Cole noticed a photographer taking their

pictures as they played. Roy stood off to one side keeping tabs. When they paused, a call reached across the field.

"Boys?"

The photographer motioned to them. Roy did the same. They ran over.

"Do you mind if I take your picture? The three of you posing together, I mean. Not an action shot."

Kenny answered for all three. "Sure."

"Okay, stand here with the trees and the mountain in the background. You, the tall one, get in the middle."

Cole got in a line with Kenny to his left and Timmy on the other side of Kenny. Cole felt Kenny's sweaty arm on his bare shoulder. Out of the corner of his eye he could see Timmy holding the football. The photographer fiddled with the lens and raised the camera.

"Now smile, everyone."

Cole smiled. The photographer shot off a series of pictures in quick succession.

"That was great, boys. Thanks."

The evening showers were a benefit to the entire ward. Cole and the other two boys were feeling grimy, so getting clean was a godsend. Everyone else on the ward felt the same way because Cole and the other two boys *smelled* grimy.

Cole also needed time to process what he'd seen when he and Kenny went to dinner. They ended up reviewing the event in the dorm after lights out. Timmy even joined the chat, sitting cross-legged on the edge of Cole's bed. Cole was sorry they couldn't include Cynthia in the conversation. Her perspective would've been helpful. Cole hadn't been ready to talk about it earlier, though, and it wouldn't have done any good anyway. Cynthia remained uncommunicative. She seemed to have barely enough energy to nod hello or eat a few bites of food.

Timmy wasn't with them on their trip to the kitchen and then to the women's ward, so Cole filled him in.

"When we left the women's ward after dropping off their stuff, I started seeing my dream over and over again. It went super fast, so it was like seconds and then start over again."

"What dream?" Timmy said. His face was barely visible in the dark.

Oh, right. He'd only told Kenny on the way down to the basement to find Daniel. So Cole rehashed the dream he'd had earlier that afternoon.

"Anyway, yesterday I saw the ghost of the nurse run from the third floor and up to the fourth. This afternoon, I dreamed I saw what happened to her through her eyes. It was like I was *her*. It was crazy. She was being chased by the Creeper, and the Creeper pushed her through a window on the fourth floor."

"Wow," Timmy said.

Cole resumed his story, reliving it yet again.

They'd left the women's ward after delivering dinner and were about to return to the elevator with the cart. As he turned to go, Cole experienced a rush of fear that almost made him tumble over. Out of nowhere, Cole was staring into the face of the Creeper, just like in his dream. The haunted, lifeless eyes. The shredded and hanging skin. He turned and ran to the stairs, fell once, and sprinted to the fourth floor.

The vision stopped. Just like that. He was still standing in the third-floor corridor with Daniel and Kenny. Cole hadn't moved or run anywhere.

"Hey?" Kenny's voice called as if miles away. Cole nodded and tried to shake off the hellish vision.

Then, like a lightning bolt, the vision resumed again—from the beginning.

The Creeper's face.

Fleeing to the stairs.

Falling, dislocating his thumb.

Scrambling up the stairs again.

Reaching the fourth floor.

Finding the alcove and seeing the windows.

And then being pushed with tremendous force through the windows.

Back on the third floor. Cole took a step toward the stairs. He turned to Daniel and Kenny. "I gotta check on something upstairs. I'll be right back. I swear." He sprinted to the stairs and took them two at a time. He made sure that he didn't stumble on the first one.

"Cole, wait," Daniel commanded from behind.

"Sorry, I can't." He kept running and within seconds landed on the fourth floor. Behind him, Cole heard Kenny say, "Let's go check it out."

"Dammit, you two. Wait."

"C'mon, Daniel, let's go." Kenny's footfalls slapped the stairs. He was on his way up. Behind Kenny, Cole could hear Daniel mumbling to himself.

The fourth floor was pretty much what he expected. Office doors. Doctor names. There was Dr. Slaver's office. There was an office for a hospital director, an accountant, and something called Personnel Manager. All in all, not interesting or what he was looking for.

He turned and headed in the opposite direction. There was one office, and then beyond that he could see the alcove.

He'd never been up here before and yet it was *exactly* like his dream.

"Cole," Kenny hissed. "What the fuck are you doing?"

With rapid-fire speed, Cole told him about the dream.

"So, is this what you saw?"

"Yep. Exactly."

Daniel reached the top of the stairs. "Lookit, you want to get in trouble? You ain't supposed to be up here."

"Just a second, Daniel. Please? I really need to check out something." Cole strode to the alcove. "Right here. It's right here."

It was. A perfect match.

The windows were straight ahead. He was practically standing at the spot where the Creeper had grabbed the nurse (him) and pushed him through the glass and down to the ledge below.

"There. Look, Kenny. That's where the nurse crashed out the window."

Kenny came up behind him and stretched over Cole's shoulder. "That's the spot right outside our dining room window."

"That's what I'm saying. Her head split open like an egg right there. I saw it."

Cole examined the window. It was intact, of course. But then, it would've been fixed right afterward.

He pushed against the window frame, only to find it solid. Was there any indication that the nurse had been pushed to her death from this spot?

Cole thought. Kenny kept his mouth shut, and other than an exasperated sigh, Daniel too kept quiet.

The tackle by the Creeper was so forceful and the race to the window so fast that Cole couldn't remember anything that might help him. It was almost instantaneous. He was at the window, glass shattered, and then he was in flight.

No, not quite. The brutal embrace. The violent push. But... but. There was a frantic effort to stop the progress. To grab something.

The window frame.

He'd grabbed the frame while being thrust through the glass, but it was no good. His fingers slipped. His fingernail snagged a section of wood. The wood was scraped off.

Cole found the frame, reached out his left hand where it would've caught... and found nothing.

"Shit."

"What?" Kenny asked.

"I remembered my nail scraping off a piece of wood. There's nothing like that here. No scrape."

"Well, they would've fixed it," Kenny offered.

"Maybe, but..." Cole sighed and turned. "Okay, Daniel, sorry. I was so sure."

"Well, c'mon. If the nurse finds out you've been up here, then you're screwed. Not to mention me."

"Wait! She was a nurse. An adult." Cole turned back to the window. He reached higher. "And she was being carried by the Creeper."

"Boy," Daniel said. "What in God's name are you jabbering about?"

Cole slid his fingers and palm up and down the frame. Kenny did the same thing, but higher, beyond Cole's reach.

And there it was. Hiding in plain sight. The window frame had been repainted. Why hadn't he thought of that? A groove in the wood about an inch long and the width of a fingernail. The result of a last desperate attempt to stay alive.

Cole caught his breath after frantically recounting the tale. The other two boys sat quietly in the dark, patiently waiting for him to resume.

"So, that means the Creeper is real. He killed a nurse by pushing her out the window on the fourth floor. I saw her escape from the third floor to the fourth; I saw her die through her own eyes. Man, that was sick."

Kenny whispered, "Don't forget, you saw her smash her head right outside our windows."

"Yeah. Thanks for the reminder. What I can't figure out is why I'm the one seeing all this."

Timmy wiggled on the edge of Cole's bed. "That's obvious, you're a seer."

Cole groaned. "Yeah, but . . . why?"

"Dumb luck?" Kenny said.

The conversation wound down quickly. Yawns replaced words. Timmy soundlessly unfolded his legs and retreated to his bed. Cole couldn't exactly say when he departed. Kenny turned over in his own bed, springs complaining softly, his breathing becoming more relaxed.

Cole stretched out, his feet taking over the end of the bed previously occupied by Timmy. Even though the air was warm, Cole pulled the sheet up to his chin. It wasn't that he was cold. He just needed some kind of shield. He started to doze and then sleep blessedly came.

But not for the entire night.

Somebody touched him. Or some*thing.*

His eyes darted around the dorm room. Nothing immediately obvious.

With dawning horror, Cole felt the now-familiar steady

breeze through the open windows dance along his body. His top sheet was gone. He wiggled his feet. No, it wasn't there.

Somebody had moved the sheet and touched him. Did they touch his private parts? Cole slowly raised his head and heard his neck creak. His undershorts were still on, and no, he didn't think they touched him *down there*. Must've been across his belly.

Cole shuddered.

With a burst, he scampered to the end of his bed and reached over for the sheet. The edge that had been up by his neck was flat on the floor. The other end was still tucked in.

He swiped at the sheet and clasped his hand around it on the first try. Frantically, he hand-over-handed the sheet until he had the loose end and pulled it up to his neck while falling back down. His head plopped on the pillow with a healthy pat.

Cole held his breath for a second and then let it go. Heart palpitations hammered his chest at a speed he hadn't thought possible.

The room remained still, but Cole continued to scan. Something was wrong. Something was *off*.

Then he saw.

The darkness moved. Or, a part of the darkness moved. Back in the corner, away from the windows. An area that nighttime light never reached. Shadows quivered and flowed back and forth like waves in the ocean.

Guttural growls emanated from within the dark. The shadow shifted jerkily out of the corner. Rapid grunts and hollow footsteps sped in the gloom. Cole thought the figure was racing toward him, but no. It rushed for the door, which opened effortlessly on its hinges.

Cole expected to see the thing backlit by the lights in the

common room at the end of the hallway. But the lights were off, just like the last time.

The Creeper scuttled through the door and disappeared from his view before the dorm door swung closed.

Cole found himself upright in bed. He crawled backward until he sat on his pillow and leaned against the headboard. He brought his legs up to his chest and embraced them. He remained in that position until he stopped shaking. It seemed like hours but was probably only minutes.

The weird things kept happening to him. How much longer was he going to be in this stupid asylum? He was afraid to ask. Where else would he even go, though? An orphanage? Maybe this was the orphanage. God, what a thought.

He burrowed under the sheet again. The idea that the Creeper had touched his belly and chest—and that was where it did touch him, he was sure—disgusted him. He rubbed his upper body as if this would dislodge the vile sensation.

The asylum awakened in chaos moments later.

Riotous laughter erupted from the women's ward above, loud and uncontrollable. There was no happiness underscoring it, only a bitter resignation and despair. Then it transformed into a long wail and sobbing. Barely audible footsteps ran to someone's aid.

The men's wards joined in. The cries from the violent patients held no distress, only rage. They cursed the blackness and fiercely disavowed their human nature. Their yells spewed hostility and death. The men from the other ward, those who were lost and forgotten, shouted only despair and futility. These men were empty.

The women above sobbed along with the originator of the chorus. The children came next. All around Cole, they pleaded and cried. Some of the cries were heartrendingly soft.

Cole's scrunched his eyes shut. He ducked completely under the covers. He tried to shut out the noise by pressing his hands over his ears, but the intensity of the sound pierced his hands with ease.

The seer wouldn't let himself look for fear of what he'd see. But he had no choice about hearing.

No, God, no, please.

Let me go. No, no.

My baby. Who will see to my baby?

God said, God told me to.

Must wash this out. If I don't they'll die. My family will die.

He loves me. He said. Why doesn't he visit?

Please, Doctor, not that? Not that needle. I won't feel again.

My head, oh God, my head.

The voices. Stop the voices.

I am so worthless.

It feels so good. I want to take them in my hands.

Squeeze away their life.

I don't deserve to live.

I'm a sinner.

Stay away, please.

It's the Creeper, Doctor.

The Creeper will eat me next.

Where's my mother?

I want my mother.

The cries of the damned. Always the damned.

My demons. Where are they?

Kenny and Timmy didn't budge. They didn't hear any of this. Only Cole.

Then Cole, completely exhausted, slept.

14

Timmy Makes a Mess

September 1962

"TIMMY!"

The reprimand rocked Cole out of bed. He must've been at the edge of the mattress, and his startle response sent him crashing to the floor. His hip and shoulder took the brunt of the fall.

"Ow," he whispered, still disoriented. The bed seemed miles away, but he reached and climbed back up.

Now what was going on? God, what a night.

But it wasn't night. An early-morning sun shone on the room at its most mundane. Not the eerie location it had been the night before.

Timmy was crying. No, it was more than that. He was panicked. Cole couldn't help noticing how nearly identical Timmy sounded to the cries from the asylum last night.

Nurse Stern stood over his bed, shaking her finger at him. "We've talked about this. About how unnatural it is. Yet you keep doing it." She didn't exactly yell at him, but her voice was harsh and no-nonsense.

A few feet to the side, Plovac stood, hands on his hips. He was smirking, the bastard.

"Out of bed, young man." Nurse Stern grabbed Timmy's upper arm and pulled. He became dead weight in the bed. His screams pierced the dorm.

Cole sensed that the nurse's hand on his arm was unbearable for Timmy.

"Get up, you little queer." Plovac took two giant steps and was on the sprawling boy.

"Leave him alone," Cole said softly.

Nurse Stern and Plovac never heard him. They lifted Timmy out of bed. Cole groaned when he saw Timmy's underwear around his knees. White stuff was splattered on his belly. It started dripping off.

So, they'd caught him. Again. This time something bad was going to happen.

"Don't you dare get your jism on me, you little faggot."

"Leave him alone," Kenny said more loudly and bravely than Cole.

"Shut up," Plovac yelled over his shoulder. He gripped Timmy by both upper arms and dragged him along the floor. Timmy's knees took the brunt. His underpants slipped off along the way and sat crumpled by the bed.

"Leave him alone." Kenny shot up from his bed.

Cole followed his example. "Don't hurt him."

"Hey." Plovac turned and dropped Timmy, who dropped like a rock. His face slapped the floor painfully. Plovac didn't care. "Shut the fuck up." He charged Kenny and slapped him with an open palm. The boy rocked slightly but remained standing.

Plovac hesitated. He obviously hadn't expected that.

Kenny glared and clenched his fists. Cole touched his arm.

"Mr. Plovac, enough!" Nurse Stern charged between the two. "That is enough, I said. Take care of Timmy. Bring him to the shower to clean up. And report back to me. Is that clear?"

Plovac didn't move. "Crystal clear, ma'am."

"Good. Now go."

Plovac turned, grasped a sobbing Timmy, and hauled him out of the dorm.

Timmy's mouth and nose were bleeding on their way out.

§

"How long you been here, Lambert?" Cole said. They'd been outside weeding Lambert's flowerbeds in the front of the main entrance. The opportunity to help the old man had arisen right after lunch and Cole jumped at the chance. He was able to get Kenny and Cynthia outside too. Kenny didn't require any coaxing, but Cynthia was having an especially tough time after hearing about Timmy being carried out of the ward. Eventually they convinced her, and Cole was happy about that. She sat on the main steps in the sunshine.

"I've been here, let's see. What's the year now? Nineteen sixty-two? Well, now, that means going on twenty years."

Kneeling among the flowers, Cole sat back on his haunches. A trickle of sweat ran down his back. The temperatures were on the rise again, and being in the sun wasn't helping. "Twenty years? Wow."

Kenny rose to his feet with a handful of weeds. He walked to a small metal bucket and tossed the bedding waste into the accumulating pile of weeds. "How do you stand it?"

Lambert's chuckle rumbled in his chest and trailed off into a cough. "Well, it ain't been bad for me. Three squares and a comfortable bed. My mind ain't the clearest, so I've been safe here. Felt like it, anyways."

"Lambert," Kenny said. "You're the sanest person I know."

This time Lambert's laugh erupted like a geyser. When he settled down, he said, "Son, you must know some really crazy people then. Either that or you don't know many at all."

"Where's Timmy, you reckon?" Cole said. The issue was weighing on his mind—like it was on everyone else's.

"Well, like I said before. I think he went for a shock treatment." Lambert sat on a wooden crate, doing a little weeding but mostly presiding over the activity. Cole didn't mind helping while the old man did the bare minimum. He was getting old; he had to be at least sixty.

"That was this morning," Kenny said. "Maybe five or six hours ago. Cole wasn't gone that long the other day."

Of course, there was no way for Cole to confirm that. He'd been so disoriented afterward that it could've been days. In fact, it really was two days before he starting feeling like himself.

"I'm worried about him," Cynthia said. These were the first words she had spoken today. Cole considered them a step in the right direction.

"So am I," Cole said.

"I understand. It's nerve-racking. But any number of things might've happened. Maybe the doctor wanted him to have something to eat first. Or maybe the doctor was delayed. Heck, he could still be sitting downstairs waiting."

Lambert was trying to be reassuring, but it wasn't working. Really, it was all guesswork. None of them had any idea what was going on.

"He didn't do so well the last time. Remember?" Cynthia said.

"Yeah," Kenny said. "He hid in the dorm and wouldn't talk to anybody. He made noises like Beatrice. It took forever for him to snap out of it. And nothing really changed. Not like it did for Cole."

"Have I changed?" Cole said.

Kenny squatted like a catcher waiting for a pitch. "I mean, I didn't know you for a long time before. But you were worried about the demons when you first got here. Now you're not. At least not as much."

That was true, more or less. He hadn't thought of the demons, although last night he'd wondered if they might've been hanging around in the back of his mind, ready to pounce.

"I guess."

"Some patients are helped by that contraption," Lambert said. "It beats what they used to do."

"What'd they used to do?" Cole asked.

"The worst was something called a, let me get this straight, a low-bot-omy. That's where they stick an ice pick above your eye and into your brain. Then they jiggle it around and slice it up some." Lambert scanned the group. "The people who had it done didn't turn out too good. Oh, they were a sight calmer afterwards, but not much of theirselves was left."

"Ugh, that's sick," Cole said.

"They still do that here?"

Lambert turned to Kenny. "No, son. They haven't done it for a while."

Cole thought about the basement rooms. "Was that done in those rooms by the shock treatment room?"

"Yep. Same area."

"Shit. Damn." Kenny shook his hand. "Dammit. I cut my hand."

Lambert stood and strolled over. "How'd you do that?" He took Kenny's hand and inspected it. "Doesn't look too bad. Rub some spit on it."

"Look," Kenny said as he inspected the area he'd been weeding. With his other hand he lifted the remnants of a glass soda bottle. "What's this doing here?"

"Gosh darnit," Lambert said. "Some fool threw a bottle into the flowers. Lazy bum couldn't use a trash can. Let's put it in the bucket. I'll deal with it later."

"Here's another piece," Kenny announced, holding up another chunk.

"Oh boy. Any more? Check. Be careful."

Kenny dug a bit more, then sat back. "That's it."

"Here. Give it to me. I'll take care of it." Cynthia took a step into the flowers and held both hands out.

Lambert passed the first piece to her. "Careful," he said. He did the same with the second shard after Kenny passed it to him.

Cynthia retreated and tossed the glass into the metal bucket, which clanged at the impact. She rubbed her hands on the seat of her pants.

"I wonder what kinda soda it was," Cole said.

"I think it was Pepsi." Cynthia checked her own hands after wiping.

They worked in silence for a few more minutes. Lambert returned to his box and Cynthia to her spot on the stairs.

Cynthia looked a little better, Cole thought. She wasn't as drawn. That made him feel a little better.

"Cole," Lambert said. "The sorrow you heard last night was all the people who died here or became so damaged that they never got better."

Cole straightened without realizing it. He stood up and stared at Lambert. Out of the corner of his eye, he could see Kenny looking at him.

"How'd you know I heard that?"

Lambert shook his head. "You keep forgetting about me."

Cole was exasperated. "I know you're a seer," he snapped. "I just didn't know we saw the same thing. You never said that."

"Now calm down, my boy. No need for anger. We don't usually see the same thing. But last night, all the lost souls done woke up. I couldn't help but notice. Your granny said you was like a radio receiver. She's right. And you're a brand new one with all the latest gadgets. You're powerful, son."

"But—"

"But nothing. You're strong. They sense you and they trust you. They want you to know."

"Know what?" Cole shook slightly.

"Know that they was alive. That they was once real. With real lives and real feelings."

"Wait a sec," Kenny said. "What good is that? I mean, so what?"

"It only takes one to remember."

Cole knelt back down. He didn't know what the old man was saying. Maybe this was just crazy talk.

Cole started to feel the pressure in his head. He had been worried because he couldn't make sense of what was happening. Now he could add another worry to that one. He had a hunch that the demons were starting to come back. Kenny just had to say what he did before. He might've jinxed the whole thing.

∾

Dale had returned from his days off. He barely nodded to them when they came in from gardening.

"You two are ripe," Dale said as he walked past them toward the nurses' station. He carried a folder and some loose sheets of paper.

"Man, we were weeding," Kenny said.

"You should wash up before you get dinner." Then he was inside the glassed-in station and plopping down at the desk. Normally they could count on some verbal give-and-take with Dale. Not today.

Cole and Kenny exchanged glances and Kenny shrugged. Cynthia chewed on a thumbnail.

"Something's wrong."

All three turned toward the common room. Laura Jean was in her usual fetal position on the couch. She looked even more haggard than the day Cole saw her as a reanimated corpse, if that was possible.

"What, Laura Jean?" Cynthia said.

"People are coming and going, looking jumpy. Nurses and staff, mostly. Although there was some guy here before who I've never seen."

Kenny marched to the nurses' station and planted himself in the doorway. "Where's Timmy?"

Cole eased up behind him. He was scared. Cynthia remained where she was, her eyes clouding over.

Dale rifled through a metal filing cabinet. His back was to them. "Still downstairs," he said over his shoulder.

Timmy should've been back by now.

Heart pounding in his chest, Cole gripped Kenny's shoulder—his nails seemed to dig right through his T-shirt. Laura Jean was right. There was something wrong. Something bad happened. A memory of Timmy's screams echoed in his head.

Kenny pressed further. "C'mon, Dale. Where's Timmy?"

The ward door opened behind them and Nurse Stern stood before them. She placed her hands on Cole and gently moved him aside. Her hands were shaking.

"Boys. Why don't you go sit in the common room?" Nurse Stern pressed on Kenny's back gently, and he shifted for her to enter the nurses' station door.

Nurse Stern circled a desk and pulled out a chair. Her face was ghastly pale with red splotches on her cheeks and neck. She looked like she'd blushed on only small portions of her face. She had never looked like this—she was always in charge and unflappable.

"Dale, man, is he okay?" Kenny persisted.

Dale stopped what he was doing and turned to see their faces. Nurse Stern also looked up. She opened her mouth and closed it again. Dale did the same thing and added a single shake of his head.

They knew. All three of them knew at the exact same moment.

Cole's eyes swelled and tears spilled over his lower lids.

Kenny swore under his breath.

Cynthia moaned, turned on her heels, and fled to her room.

When Kenny and Cole delivered dinner to the women's

unit, a few of the ladies tried to comfort them. There were a few *I'm sorrys*, and Mrs. D hugged both of them. This violation of the no-touching rule was overlooked by the nurse working that shift on the ward.

"Tell him he was loved when you see him," Mrs. D whispered to Cole as she pulled away.

Standing off to the side of the community room for the ward was Plovac. He stood silently and stared at both him and Kenny, his face was taut with some emotion Cole couldn't read. He could've been mad or afraid, but he was trying to look as menacing as he could.

Cole was jolted with a thought. Could Plovac have done something to hurt Timmy? As a warning to the other kids about not telling anyone about what he did to Cynthia?

That didn't make any sense. Why hurt Timmy? He wouldn't say anything.

Dinner in the kids' ward was miserable.

Cole and Kenny sat together eating quietly. The dinner, which Cole couldn't remember five minutes after finishing, had no taste. Cynthia wouldn't come out of her room. The seat where Timmy typically sat was heartrending in its emptiness.

After dinner, Dale talked to whoever was interested about Timmy. Sitting in the common room, he described what happened. It turned out Timmy died of a brain aneurism. He'd had a blood vessel in his brain that was weak. Sometime after the shock treatment, the blood vessel burst and he died. The chance of this happening was like one in a million.

"The shock didn't kill him?" Cole said.

Dale shook his head. "Could it have played a part? We'll never know. But Timmy's blood vessel was a ticking time bomb. It could've gone anytime."

None of this made sense. How could sending all those volts through a person's head not hurt him in some way?

At some point, Dale left the room to go to the nurses' station. The television was on in the common room, but no one watched. Kenny played solitaire and Cynthia still remained in her room. After about an hour, Cole went back to the dorm to get his book about the orphans living in the boxcar. He needed something to get his mind off his suffocating depression.

On the way to the boys' dorm, Cole found himself counting steps. This wasn't a complete surprise. The news about Timmy had resulted in a renewed effort by the demons. They were threatening to explode from his consciousness and take over the ward.

He'd lose control. He'd be, like, taken over. And that would be terrible.

Counting *26-27-28* steps to the side table at his bed, he picked up the book and turned to go back to the community room.

Timmy stood in his path.

The dead boy's mouth was working but no words came out.

The Boxcar Children slipped from Cole's fingers and fell to the floor.

"Timmy? What?"

Timmy's lips moved, but still no sound. Cole stepped closer and Timmy started to fade.

No!

Again the lips moved. Timmy's face became frantic. One arm lifted and pointed in the direction of the common room.

Cole saw it then. Timmy's lips forming a word. *Cynthia*.

And he wasn't pointing to the common room, but the girls' hallway.

Cole ran for the nurses' station, his book forgotten on the floor.

15

Three Boys in a Photo

August, Present Day

"BEING ON THE PEDIATRIC WARD was tough on kids."

A few chuckles and grins.

"It wasn't all terrible, though. This was a picture taken by a reporter who did a story for a now-defunct regional magazine." Chaz picked up the remote and turned on the common room's screen. Moments later, a picture appeared.

The picture showed three boys who looked hot and sweaty. One had thrown his T-shirt over his shoulder while another, clearly the youngest of the three, had tucked his shirt into the back of his pants. A third boy, probably the second oldest, had a football tucked under his arm. The oldest boy's arm rested on the youngest boy's shoulder. All were sporting shy grins.

Chaz surveyed the group. The kids gaped with fascinated expressions. They likely were wondering what it would be like to live in a place like this without their parents.

The others looked wistful, with the old dude staring intently.

"The one in the middle is cute," said one college girl to the other.

"He certainly is," one of the wives added. The husbands groaned.

"When was this taken?" the mom asked.

"Early sixties, I think," Chaz said. He looked at Evie.

"Nineteen sixty-two," Evie said.

"We've got some recordings that we'd like to share with you," Chaz said. He picked something off a lower shelf. "This," he said, holding up a rectangular object that looked vaguely like a two-way radio, "is called a ghost box. Another name for it is spirit box."

Chaz felt embarrassed bringing this out. The contraption was the stupidest thing ever.

"This device allows us to contact ghosts by making use of radio frequencies. When you turn it on, it makes radio-frequency sweeps to create white noise. In theory, the white noise gives the ghost enough energy they need to be heard by us. What you hear is the voice coming through the static, the white noise, as they try to talk to us."

This was a load of crap, even for a ghost-hunting fanatic like Chaz. Basically the damn thing was a radio scanner. He'd tried to explain this to Evie months ago when he brought her his dad's old-fashioned radio from home. "Look," he said. "I can recreate what we get on that dumb thing by turning the knob up and down the dial. You zip across the frequencies, and you can capture static and fragments of talk or music."

He demonstrated. Bursts of white noise, pops, familiar yet unidentifiable sounds, musical notes, and portions of words jumped from the tinny speaker. She still wasn't convinced, and there was nothing he could say to talk her out of her belief. She remained enamored by the piece-of-shit "ghost box." He gave up after that. He didn't want her getting pissed at him.

Nonetheless, he knew why people were fooled. Traces of speech were often picked up within the static. As anybody who'd taken an Introduction to Psychology class knew, the brain was pretty good at trying to fill in the missing details of any stimulus it received. So the ghost box would present some snippet of a word and the brain would try to make sense of it. If it couldn't, and someone else provided an interpretation, *eureka*. Yes, it fits! That's what I heard!

Much to his shame, Chaz was going to demonstrate this right now.

He turned on the ghost box. The thing scanned the frequencies, spitting static and an occasional word spoken by a radio announcer on the AM dial. People turned toward him for a reaction whenever they heard something that sounded like speech. Chaz only shook his head in response. After a minute or so of meaningless shit, he turned off the gadget. Some folks somewhere were making a ton of money selling these things on the internet for a hundred dollars and more.

"It's very hard to differentiate natural sounds that occur across radio frequencies. They could be anything."

The old dude piped up. "I thought some of those ghosts had professional-sounding voices."

Chaz laughed with the group. "That's it exactly. You're picking up DJs, talk radio, commercials. Right from a regional radio station."

The crowd look disappointed. Evie gave him a dirty look, as she usually did at this point of the tour.

"However, sometimes something strange does occur. Take a look. Or, actually, take a listen." He advanced beyond the picture of the boys and went to a black screen. "This is a recording of a ghost box during a radio-frequency sweep. It's mostly just static, but there's a brief interjection of something. The clip's only ten seconds long. See if you can pick it up."

The thing was, nobody could pick it up—much to Evie's chagrin. They had a running bet about whether anyone would ever hear the word. Chaz didn't think it would happen.

He pushed play on the remote. Ten seconds of static. Nothing from the group.

"That's it?"

"I didn't hear a thing."

"Are you making this up?"

Chaz held up his hand. "Okay, wait. Let me play it again."

He did. Same reactions. No one heard anything.

Time to fill them in and restore some of Evie's dignity. "Now, I was like you. I couldn't hear it. But Evie did."

Heads turned predictably in her direction. She took over.

"I definitely heard something when I first heard it. Chaz and I argue about this all the time, so if you catch any looks from us, that's why."

Chaz was amused that she'd been admitting to this in recent tours. It made them feel a true team, somehow.

"What I did is add a caption at the bottom of the screen. See if you can hear the word once you read what it is."

Of course they would. They always did.

Evie advanced the screen, and the same static jumped to life. At the right moment, a word appeared on the screen. Once it did, everyone made their own sound. Some gasps, some oohs and aahs. Evie started the clip again. The word appeared on the screen, and everyone recognized the slight blip in the static and a young person's voice saying, "Timmy."

"Who's Timmy?" the mom said.

"He probably was a patient here. One of the kids since we're in the pediatric ward," Chaz said.

"I think your coworker is right," Baldy said. "It's clear as a bell now."

Evie playfully stuck her tongue out at Chaz, much to the delight of the kids.

"We don't know who he is or whether that's his voice. Some people think it's another kid calling to him, while others think it's Timmy introducing himself."

"I bet that's Timmy telling us his name," said the oldest kid.

"Young man," said the old dude. "I think you're right." He smiled at the kid.

"One thing we do know is that Timmy likes to play ball." Chaz swirled his head, looking for a prop that he just realized was missing.

"It's in the dining room. In the corner." Evie ran off and returned seconds later with a kickball. Chaz motioned for her to continue.

"We've been able to play ball with Timmy every once in a while. It hardly ever happens, but we try this every time we're in here. We always film, hoping for the best, and we'll show you an example in a moment." Evie took a step backward to look down the hall. "Everyone come here, please."

The crowd pressed in closer to her. She pointed.

"Down there was the boys' dormitory. That's where Timmy seems to hang out. I'm going to roll the ball down there, and we'll see if he's in the mood to play. If he is, he'll roll the ball right back. The few times it's happened were almost right away, so we won't have to wait long. Ready?" She looked to the group. The kids gathered to the front to see clearly.

"Okay, here goes."

Evie gently rolled the ball down into the boys' dorm. As it slowed, it sideswiped a bedframe, softly changed direction, and stopped.

They waited.

Sadly, nothing happened. The sighs were audible.

Chaz advanced the screen. "Take a look here." Heads turned and Chaz hit Play. A clip appeared showing Evie roll the ball like she'd just done live. It stopped in the room, not hitting anything this time. A heartbeat later, the ball rolled backward down the hall toward Evie and came to a stop after traveling five or six feet.

The group clapped.

"That's the only time me and Evie have seen it. We cheered like fans at a football game right after a touchdown."

"All right, wait," Potbelly said. "That's impressive, but has there ever been a more forceful roll? I mean, could that've been from a defect in the floor or a breeze from a window."

Chaz deliberated, as he had many times in the past. "I know what you mean. Something a little more robust would be more convincing. But still. Think about it. The ball came to a complete stop. Only then did it roll in the opposite direction for five feet. That's impressive."

Chaz *was* impressed, too. He'd never witnessed anything more dramatic.

"And the floor is level, by the way. We checked. Could it have been the wind? Maybe, but the air was quite calm that day."

The questions shifted to Timmy. Who was he? What happened to him? Neither Chaz nor Evie had satisfactory answers.

"The only thing we really know about him, based on the

lore passed down over the years, was his skill at sports. Hence his sporadic effort to play ball."

Chaz and Evie ushered the tour down into the boys' dormitory area. Evie began the next commentary.

"This section is unique. You'll notice that the boys didn't have their own rooms. Instead they had this open-style dorm. See the windows all around in a fan shape? The heads of the beds were under the windows. Depending on the year, they could've had six or seven beds in here."

The crowd broke apart and wandered around the room. The three couples floated over to the windows to check out the view ("Very nice"). The two younger kids got on their hands and knees to check under the beds. Most of the beds were just frames, although a couple maintained a musty-looking mattress for the visual effect. The older boy picked up the ball and bounced it a few times until his mother asked him to please stop.

The old dude stood over the first bed and lightly touched the mattress. Chaz shuddered. There was an assortment of stains decorating the center, the nature of which he hated to speculate on. The old dude didn't seem troubled by them, though. He pursed his lips and stared at the bed before running his fingers along the metal frame.

Chaz gave them a few moments to explore before resuming his presentation.

"Two things about this dormitory," he said. The old dude looked up into the room as if he'd been lost in thought. "The first involves a tragic story. We're not sure when this happened, but evidently one of the boys was taken by the janitor and brought into a basement tunnel, which we'll see a little later." Here, Chaz had to be careful given the age of the kids. "The story goes that the janitor, whose name was Daniel, killed the boy down there after he, well, you get the idea."

The oldest kid asked, "You mean he sexually assaulted the boy?"

"Uh, yeah. That's what I mean." Chaz glanced at Evie, who could only raise her eyebrows in reply. The kid's parents didn't seem particularly concerned. They'd probably covered this topic at home.

Evie stepped into the center of the room, right next to the college girls who had been scanning the area while rotating in place. "Anyway, that event, or the tale surrounding the event, gave rise over time to folklore about the Creeper."

"The Creeper?" One of the husbands, Chaz didn't catch which one.

"That's creepy," the Beard's wife said. Everyone chuckled.

"Yes, the Creeper," Evie said. "The story morphed some over the decades, but whatever it was, the kids were especially afraid of it. The Creeper was some kind of an evil spirit. And the creepiest part"—here Evie emphasized *creepiest*—"was that the Creeper would snatch kids out of their bed, take them to the tunnel in the basement, and eat them." The last two words were whispered, and Evie relished drawing them out in a spooky way.

Naturally, the crowd followed suit with exaggerated whispers and shudders. Par for the course. They had the crowd eating out of their hands.

"So, was there a Creeper character?" one of the college girls asked for the group.

"There were reports of people seeing him. Many from right in this room. You could see how the story became folklore over time. And how it might have sprung from the account of Daniel murdering the boy."

Potbelly squawked loudly and flinched, which made a number of others jump and squeal.

"Kevin, what?" His wife was alarmed.

The guy tried to laugh it off, but he wasn't convincing. His eyes darted among the group. "Sorry, jeez. I swear to God, I could've sworn somebody grabbed my shoulder."

The rest of the party stood and gaped at him.

"I'm not joking."

"Kevin, bro." This was Baldy.

"Which brings me to the second feature of this room," Chaz said. "Daniel haunts it. At least that's the speculation. The most frequent target on our tours is a male—regardless of age."

"Justin, come here," the Mom said, calling the oldest boy to her side. The other two kids were already near her.

"Mom," Justin said with a groan. Still, he complied.

Chaz continued. "A common experience is for males to feel a disembodied touch or a grab. Sometimes the door to the dorm will close before someone is touched. That didn't happen tonight, though."

Everyone turned to see that the door was still ajar.

"Have you ever felt Daniel?" Potbelly said.

Chaz expected Potbelly was hoping to save face by finding someone who shared the same experience. He was happy to oblige.

"Last July. I'd brought a stepladder in to close an upper window. I was a few steps up when the door shut on its own. And, yeah, I knew the story. At the time, though, I was just frustrated because it was hot and the window was stuck. Then a hand clasped my leg. Right above the knee. I was wearing shorts, and I could feel the cold sensation on my skin. Let me tell you, that gave me goosebumps."

"No pictures, though?" the dad asked.

"Sorry, no. Just what's in my memory."

16

Not a Good Place
for Kids

September 1962

COLE RAGED IN HIS RESTRAINTS.

Plovac and Dale had put him in a straightjacket, something he'd never heard of before. He hated it so much. Both of his hands, which were wrapped around his torso, burned with pins and needles. For the past few hours, Cole didn't know how many, he'd been strapped to a gurney in the basement.

Kenny was on a different gurney but without a straightjacket. They'd given him a shot of something that knocked him out cold. Still, five straps kept him in place.

Cole let loose with a scream, probably his tenth since he'd been locked in this room. His voice was getting hoarse. Since his head was the only part of his body he could move, he resorted to banging it repeatedly on the gurney. The result was a resounding headache that prompted him to stop. The only thing left to do was cry and swear.

Shit, shit, shit. Oh God.

He cried some more.

Seeing Timmy's ghost in the dorm room had set things in motion.

"We gotta check on Cynthia. Timmy said," Cole hollered as he ran into the common room.

Kenny jumped to his feet and bumped the table where he'd been playing cards. The deck went flying. "Let's go." Kenny sprinted for the girls' corridor. Cole was relieved that Kenny didn't question him like an adult would.

"Boys! Wait!" Dale flew out of the nurses' station in pursuit of Cole. His long strides almost caught up—Cole could feel him practically on top of him. Any instant now a hand would clasp his shoulder and pull him back.

The door separating the hall from the common room never had a chance to swing closed as the three pounded it open in rapid succession.

"Kenny, stop right now, dammit," Dale yelled.

Kenny applied the brakes at Cynthia's door, but he slid on the floor in his stocking feet and passed the entrance. He recovered and tried to turn the knob, but his hand slipped. Cole ran into him at nearly full speed and both tumbled to the floor.

"Now, stay there," Dale said, a few registers louder than his regular tone. Dale turned the knob.

"Cynthia, knock knock." Dale entered and stopped after one step.

"What is it?" Kenny said.

Dale's shoulders tensed. "Oh, no."

"What?"

Dale stepped backwards and turned to face the two of them sitting on the floor. He tried to grab the door and close it behind him but missed the knob completely. Cynthia's door remained ajar.

"I need you two boys to return to the common room, please."

"Why, what happened?" Kenny said. When Dale didn't respond, Kenny raised his voice. "Cynthia, are you okay? Cynthia?"

"I need you to go to the common room, please," Dale ordered with a trembling voice.

Behind Dale, Beatrice walked silently down the corridor. Dale didn't even notice her coming. When she was right behind Dale, she twisted to look beyond the door to Cynthia's room. She gasped, and Dale's eyebrows rose up when he realized that she was behind him.

Then she screamed.

Dale tried to herd her from the corridor, but she collapsed against a wall. Dale pleaded with her to leave as he physically tried to force her back to the common room. The girl's arms rocketed upward and cradled her head.

With the door still ajar and unguarded, Kenny took a chance and crawled to Cynthia's room. Cole scampered behind him.

"Oh fuck," Kenny said.

Cole could only bring his hands to his mouth.

Cynthia was sprawled on the floor. Her shirt was drenched in blood that had long since dried. Blood had cascaded from her body and created a pool that rippled unevenly along the floor. Sprayed blood also decorated one wall.

Both of Cynthia's arms had been sliced open, starting at her wrists and continuing up her forearm. A shard of glass sparkled on the floor nearby—one of the pieces they'd found in the garden earlier. Cynthia must've palmed it and hid it in her pants pocket.

The straps hadn't budged with Cole's thrashing. They hadn't even loosened. His jaw ached as a result of gritting his teeth in frustration.

He ceased his straining and just cried. The straightjacket was so damnably infuriating and he couldn't do anything.

Worse still was the building pressure outside his field of vision. Or maybe it was inside his head. He could no longer tell. But the demons were back, taunting him, ready to pounce.

Back to counting. Cole turned his head and noticed the tiles on the wall. Those might work. Each row was staggered half of a tile from the rows above and below it. He could follow one without getting confused.

He counted the first few quickly but slowed and mouthed the higher numbers out loud *10-11-12-13.*

Damn.

That's all he could see lying down. Cupboards also obstructed his view. He moved to the row above and had more success. He counted to twelve.

The pressure eased, but didn't dissipate completely.

H-E-A-V-E-N. He visualized his heaven scene and recounted, emphasizing the number six.

"Your demons are back, I guess."

Cole flinched not expecting to hear anybody. He must've spoken aloud. Kenny was awake when he swiveled his head to check.

"Yeah, they are. Are you okay?" Cole's eyes and cheeks were wet from his crying. His voice was croaky.

Kenny stared at the ceiling and exhaled. "I've been coming

to for a couple of minutes. The stuff wore off, and besides, you've been making so much noise."

"Sorry."

Kenny shrugged, or at least it seemed like he tried to under the straps. "Worst case, we get our brains fried. And we do a lot of sleeping for the next day or so." The more he talked, the more he sounded groggy.

Cole's heart rocked in his chest. He scanned the room for the first time. A dim light was on somewhere behind them. He pictured a desk lamp for some reason but couldn't really tell. They were in a basement room. A small rectangular window was positioned high on the wall above Kenny's gurney, flush with the ceiling. Cole visualized the ground just below the window outside in his mind. He wished he was on the other side of that window. No daylight shone through, so it was still nighttime. Or early morning.

The briefest flicker of light flashed beyond the glass. It was so quick that Cole wondered if he'd imagined it. But he hadn't. It was lightning. Heat lightning, most likely.

"What's this room?" Cole said. The walls above the tiles were painted a baby-blue color.

"Recovery room, I think. We're just down the hall from the shock treatment room." Kenny said this with little emotion. It was like he wasn't alarmed at all.

"So that's why you think we're going to get shocked?"

"Yeah, what else? We lost our cool upstairs. It'll be justifiable in their minds."

Cole reflected on this. "But Cynthia's dead. So's Timmy. What did they expect?"

Kenny turned his head. "They see everything we do as part of our craziness. Doesn't matter if there's a rational explanation."

Cole thought back to a few hours ago—when they found Cynthia in her room.

The smell coming from her room was sweet and coppery. And sickening. There was an undercurrent of foul spoilage. She hadn't been dead so long that she'd smell bad, Cole knew that much, but still a reeking aroma filled the air.

Cole turned his head and took a deep breath so he wouldn't puke. This only helped a little, so he scooted on his butt out of the doorframe. Kenny kept staring, but breathed rapidly through his nose.

Laura Jean stepped out of her room. If anything, she looked even more like a skeleton than she had a few days ago. She leaned her back against the wall and propelled slowly in their direction, using her forward arm to pull and the other to push.

"Laura Jean," Cole said, shaking his head slowly.

She ignored him. Her eyes were filmy, almost pale, and gazed out of desperately dark sockets. Her complexion was like curdled cream; clumps of stringy hair hung listlessly from her head. When she was almost near enough to peer into Cynthia's room, she pushed weakly against the wall and stood on spindly legs. Cole expected them to snap like pencils.

"Oh." Barely a murmur.

She leaned backward and lost her balance, crashing into the wall, and slid awkwardly to the floor. Cole could've sworn he heard bones crack.

"Dale!"

A rustle of activity from the common room. Dale appeared from around the corner on the run and almost stumbled when he saw what was before him.

"Aw, shit."

Dale slowed his pace when he was within a few feet of them, knelt down, and began giving instructions.

"I know you're upset, but I need your help. I need for you to go to the common room and give Beatrice some company. Please don't drive her into worse shape by talking about what you saw in front of her."

Cole said okay under his breath but Kenny asked, "What're you going to do?"

"Somebody's got to attend to Laura Jean. Then I'm gonna call for help."

The wait in the common room was interminable. Kenny sat seething in a wooden desk chair. His expression was stony, and he glared unblinking at the entrance to the ward. Sweat beaded on his forehead, his skin flushed as if embarrassed. If anyone so much as touched his shoulder, he'd probably detonate. Cole had not seen him this angry and focused. He was waiting for someone to enter, and Cole had a decent idea who.

Dale spent ten minutes running between the hallway and the nurses' station. He must've traveled back and forth three times. He made urgent phone calls while in the station and took care of Laura Jean. It appeared that he had at least helped her back to her room.

Beatrice was rocking in her seat, and the motion was becoming more intense. Her distress was driving Cole insane. He ended up finding papers and crayons for the both of them to color. Her rocking slowed down. Within a minute or two it stopped altogether as she became absorbed in scribbling with a red crayon. Cole wondered if this was supposed to be Cynthia's blood.

The first person on the floor was Nurse Stern, quickly followed by Dr. Slaver. The shrink barreled right past them as if they were invisible. Nurse Stern paused long enough to approach Cole. "Are you okay?"

Cole knew she was asking him and not Beatrice, but he answered for both of them. "No. Beatrice went nuts. I don't feel so good either."

"I know. This is terrible." Then she sidestepped away and went to Kenny. "I'm so sorry, Kenny."

Kenny's eyes flickered from the doorway and sought her face. He blinked once, and Cole thought for a moment that he might cry. But he didn't. He just looked madder.

Nurse Stern reached out her hand, hesitated for a beat, and touched his shoulder. Kenny flinched a little, then relaxed. Nurse Stern tore away and bolted for the girls' corridor. She moved faster than Cole thought possible.

Three aides in white uniforms burst into the ward. Two were navigating a gurney. Cole recognized one of them as the acne-scarred guy who'd assisted with his shock treatment. None noticed them sitting in the common room.

Cole turned back to Beatrice, who was still furiously drawing slashes of red. Sections of the paper were starting to crinkle; soon it would rip. When that happened, he'd have to think of something else to keep Beatrice occupied.

Kenny stood abruptly in Cole's peripheral vision. Cole practically jumped at the suddenness of his move. Kenny's face was a shade of red only slightly lighter than Beatrice's coloring. His hands clenched in fists at his sides. His knuckles were white.

"You did this," said Kenny.

Cole rotated in his chair.

Plovac stood in the doorway. His smarmy grin sent Cole's blood boiling. The pressure soared in his head and a presence mushroomed outside the range of his vision. Cole focused his attention on a window and let his eyes scan the four sides of the frame, counting as he went. He traced the pattern over and over and continually counted *1-2-3-4*. He'd get to the point of relaxing a little, but then he'd be drawn to the showdown between the bastard Plovac and Kenny.

"You killed her."

"You're confused, boy. I've been working a different ward all day. Nowhere near the little twat." Plovac flexed his shoulder muscles under his close-fitting white button-down short-sleeved shirt.

"You sick fucker."

Kenny stepped forward. He somehow seemed cool and calm as if he was in church. He took another step, turned to skirt Beatrice's chair, then resumed. His steps were smooth and measured.

Plovac's head twitched. Cole thought he saw a second's worth of fear in his expression; it was replaced with a shit-eating grin.

"Sick fucker." Kenny took two more steps. "Pervert. Kiddy diddler."

Kenny didn't quicken his pace or slow it down. Plovac took out some kind of rubber baton when Kenny was within five feet. A nightstick.

"Enough of this shit." Plovac raised his hand and brought the baton down toward Kenny's head. The weapon never connected.

Kenny's left arm shot up and deflected it.

Plovac looked shocked, but before he could bring his baton up a second time, Kenny shoved him. Plovac's arms flew out like he was going to fly. The nightstick sailed from his hand and landed harmlessly on the floor. Plovac screamed before his body cracked against the doorframe.

"You raped her. You killed her." Kenny was loud, but the yelling was measured, not uncontrolled.

The aide regained his balance, charged Kenny, and grabbed him in a bear hug.

Cole rose from his chair and ran toward the struggle. Beatrice started bellowing.

"Leave him alone," Cole yelled, joining the melee. He clasped one of Plovac's arms and tried to pull it loose. He only succeeded in annoying Plovac, who released Kenny long enough to slap Cole with the back of his hand. Cole fell against the couch and toppled to the floor.

By this time, the ruckus had drawn the other staff from the hallway. Kenny was squirming out of Plovac's grip. Plovac had Kenny by his T-shirt, which was stretched to the ripping point.

Cole jumped to his feet again and ran to help Kenny. He threw himself at Plovac to distract him, but the aide seized a clump of his hair and pulled. Cole screamed as he was tossed again to the side.

The other aides descended on him and Kenny. The weight of someone's body crushed him to the floor. There was tussling and flipping and Cole couldn't focus on where he was or what was happening.

Then it was over. Cole was on the couch, his arms tied across his torso in a straightjacket.

Kenny was slumped over in another chair. Dale had a syringe in his hand.

Two more gurneys appeared along with other aides and nurses.

Roy's face was close to his. "Easy, Cole." Then he was gone.

When they lifted him to a gurney he screamed and didn't stop. He couldn't.

Kenny was on the other gurney, completely knocked out.

The last image he had of the ward was Cynthia's body prone on the first gurney farther back in the girls' hall. In the common room, Beatrice was crying, and Nurse Stern was giving her a shot to calm her down.

Cole opened his eyes. The room was a little brighter. He must've dozed.

"Almost morning, I think," Kenny said. Strapped down on his back with arms and legs straight, Kenny had to be uncomfortable. His voice still had the tiniest hint of mushiness.

In the background, somewhere over the peaks of the mountains, thunder rumbled.

"I bet they're fixing to shock us this morning. Probably when Slaver comes in."

Cole tried to shift but was unable. His arms were even more asleep if that was possible. God, he hated this jacket.

A flash of light brightened the room. What seemed like a flashbulb going off was followed seconds later by thunder. The storm was getting closer.

"Like I said, I think we could end up getting fried." Kenny turned his head and stared at Cole. The silence was long enough to really catch his attention.

"What are you saying?"

"I'm saying it could happen, but if we get our chance we need to stop it." The last few words were spoken softly.

"Then what do we do?" Cole said, feeling anxious at the same time.

"We escape. We get the hell out of here."

Now Cole was scared. Assuming they escaped the building, then what did they do? Where would they go?

First things first, though.

"How do we stop it?"

"I don't know. I haven't gotten that far yet."

Cole swallowed nervously. He couldn't figure out where this was going. Outside, there was another flash of lightning.

"They'll take us both into that treatment room. And I'm going to pretend like I'm still unconscious."

Kenny yawned, and Cole couldn't help thinking it wouldn't take much acting to fake being passed out.

"Then what?"

"Maybe we'll get lucky. They have to take the straps off to move us to the table." Kenny lifted his head to check out the straps. "I'll make my move, get you, and then we take off."

The plan sounded really stupid. In fact, there was no plan. Kenny was just making it up as he went along. Cole was disappointed in his friend. There was no way out of this. They were going to get the shocks.

"Cole?"

He glowered at the ceiling and kept silent. What could he say?

"Cole?"

"What?" He didn't move.

"Look at me, okay? Please?"

Relenting, Cole turned. Kenny's head lifted off the table.

"No bullshitting with your demons. You gotta let them come out."

Cole's stomach lurched. "What? What're you talking about?"

Let the demons out?

"I'm serious. None of that crazy counting stuff. There's no demons. Only you."

Cole blew air forcefully from his mouth, trying to gain control over his nerves. What was Kenny talking about?

"Cole. Whatever you're scared of, it's inside you. There's nothing else. You hear me?"

"No."

"Bullshit. You know it. If something happens, you let them go, Cole. You fucking let them rip."

The next streak of lightning was intense. The accompanying thunder came almost on top of the flash. The crash reverberated from one end of the building to another. Metal rattled, and the building shook with the boom.

"I hear someone," Kenny whispered. "Remember, I'm still out." His entire being settled like a rag doll.

In the corridor, there were footsteps and voices. Keys rattled across the hall and a door opened. Light switches clicked on. More footsteps approached—Cole guessed there were lots of people. A man's voice gave instructions. Slaver, probably.

Imitating Kenny, Cole tried to make himself seem groggy.

The door to their room shook in its frame. Cole thought maybe it was thunder, but then the door swung open.

"Morning, boys." The voice was taunting. Overhead lights flickered. Kenny played dead. Cole looked at the door.

"Time for the show," Plovac said, and grinned like a madman.

The walk to the treatment room across the hall felt like miles. Cole's legs were wobbly, as if he had no bones in them. He feared he might trip over his own feet. Plovac would probably end up slapping him upside the head if he did.

Cole was surprised they were letting him walk, but

maybe maneuvering two gurneys across the hall and into the treatment room was too much work. Kenny lay unmoving on his gurney as they wheeled him over to the room right behind Cole. Kenny was a fantastic actor. Plovac didn't notice a thing, nor did the acne-scarred mole guy who came over to help.

Thunder had become more frequent over the last minute or two, but the loudness diminished while they were in the hallway.

Upon entering the treatment room, a chorus of screams erupted from the walls. Cole jumped as countless faces pressed against the stretching membrane of the walls.

"Stop wasting time, young man. Climb up here," Dr. Slaver said without examining Cole. The man didn't seem to care that he was just a kid. He was fiddling with the earmuff things that went on his temples.

Besides the doctor, the pleasant nurse from his last shock treatment was back. He couldn't recall her name and realized he wasn't even sure if he ever knew it. It was just the four people helping, not the crowd from last time that included Nurse Stern and another nurse.

"Turn around." Acne-scars didn't bother waiting for Cole to move; he grabbed his shoulders and roughly spun him halfway. The guy's fingers were messing with the straight-jacket. In no time the garment was off. Cole rubbed his arms.

"Up," Acne-scars said, and motioned to the table. There was a slight yet insistent push between his shoulder blades.

Cole banged his knee on the table climbing up.

"Ouch," the pleasant nurse said, smiling at him.

He did all he could to smile in return, but all he could manage was a weak one. The screeches and howls from the walls were too distracting. The cacophony pierced his ears like roofing nails. The nurse gently lowered him to his back. She moved her face closer.

"There. Try to relax." Her eyes stared into his. "Did I say last time that your eyes are a beautiful color?"

Cole nodded.

"I thought so. Sorry to sound so silly, but purple is my favorite color."

"They're violet," Cole said.

"Yes, they are. I like violet." If anything her smile became wider.

"Nurse." Dr. Slaver sounded annoyed.

"Yes, Doctor." The nurse shifted out of his view.

A series of lightning flashes produced nearly continuous illumination. Heads turned away from their focused tasks and looked upward toward the window flush with the ceiling. The room shook with a blast of thunder that kept rolling like huge trucks on the highway. Just as the shaking settled down to a minor rumble, the next streaks of lightning flashed and the process started all over.

Cole tilted his head back and saw that the sky had turned dark green—almost black. Sure, it was technically morning and the sky had been already gray, but this was *different*. The clouds were alive like a roiling mass of copperheads.

Inside the room, the lights flickered and went out for a second.

"That's just great. We may have to rely on the emergency power today," Dr. Slaver said somewhere behind Cole's head.

"Wonder how much Dale gave this kid. He's still out." Plovac stood by Kenny's side. His gurney had been rolled into the room behind Cole. Plovac lifted Kenny's arm about six inches and let go. It dropped lifelessly back to Kenny's side.

The walls had stopped wailing for Plovac's brief demonstration, the face-shaped contours focusing entirely at Kenny. As soon as Kenny's limp arm hit the table, the walls resumed their screaming. Their tone possessed a sense of urgency—like they were excited about the *possibilities.*

Did that make sense?

Yes. And he knew why. Two of the faces became distinct. Cole recognized them.

Timmy and Cynthia.

They were right in his line of sight, and their mouths were open as if preparing to speak instead of scream. Then they did. "*Be ready. Be ready. Be ready.*"

Underneath the pounding thunder came a roar. Everybody lifted their heads, trying to get a handle on the sound. The roar grew louder. White-hot lightning burst menacingly across the swampy green clouds. Gasps and curses spilled from the adults in the room.

Something beyond the everyday was happening.

Kenny maintained his act while Cole desperately tried to sort out what to do. Instantly, his demons were closer than ever. The pressure was building. Cole needed to do his rituals to keep them suppressed.

Kenny's eyes twitched. No one but Cole noticed.

You let them go, Cole. You fucking let them rip.

The demons?

There's no demons. There's only you. You're afraid of you.

"What in God's name..."

Was that Plovac? Cole couldn't tell. Demons had grouped outside his vision, behind and to the sides of his head. The faces of past patients that he could see, including his beloved Timmy and Cynthia, screamed for him to be ready.

Their keening matched the haunting sounds of the storm.

Cole tilted his head. From this angle, he saw a tree that he hadn't seen moments ago. It was twisting and hurtling in the air. It was flying. And coming closer.

Acne-scars stepped backward into the table. The guy didn't appear to notice that he'd bumped into it. An object on the man's hip drew Cole's attention. The nightstick. Just like the one that Plovac had used yesterday. Acne-scars had it in his pocket, right next to Cole's outstretched arm. His hand was practically touching it. Amazingly, it was just *there*, sitting in his pocket. Shouldn't it be attached to his belt for safekeeping?

It didn't matter. This was an opportunity, pure and simple. The chance Kenny talked about.

Cole wasn't strapped down. Neither was Kenny. They had removed his straps to move him to the table after Cole's shock treatments were finished. That was a mistake.

"I think we're safe down here." Dr. Slaver. The prick.

You let them go, Cole. You fucking let them rip.

The tree slammed into the building just above their window.

Cole reached for the nightstick. He grabbed it. He sat up and pulled back his arm.

Dr. Slaver said something in warning. No one reacted.

Cole brought his arm down like a hammer. Before he crashed Acne-scars on the back of his head, the lights wavered again. Cole didn't see the impact. He only felt it. Nerves sang with the collision.

Acne-scars slumped to his knees and groaned. No one noticed other than Slaver because utter chaos descended upon the building.

Their room shuddered. Mortars of dislodging bricks pelted the exterior walls. Gutters torn from their fasteners sliced the air and flew in random directions. Cars were overturned, leaping from their parking spaces and landing yards away. Chain-link fences were ripped from posts and flexed like rubber bands in midair. The posts turned into javelins and hurtled mindlessly into structures.

Cole saw none of this. But he knew. He was a seer.

Shattered glass imploded into rooms across the asylum—including the shock treatment room. The pleasant nurse screamed. Mud and dirt whorled across everyone.

"Stop him," Slaver yelled above the bedlam.

"You little fucker." Plovac turned on Cole, nudging Kenny's gurney.

Additional debris sailed through the window. Unbelievably, the room became darker. Cole raised his arm again, and Slaver tried to clasp it. Cole shook him off and backhanded the doctor across the nose with the nightstick. Slaver slipped harmlessly to the floor.

The malignant darkness swirled faster in the room and sent curtains, bedding, metal instruments, paper, electric cords, and God knows what else twisting in the air. Cole was slapped with papers that sliced like a razor blade.

Plovac, only feet away, fought against the unnatural stream of wind. The nurse was nowhere to be seen.

"I'm gonna kick your ass." Plovac reached for Cole and touched his shoulder.

A shadow loomed. The roar of wind and voices reached a crescendo. Cole shut his eyes as the shadow—darker than the already murky light—covered him.

"*Leave the kid alone.*"

A yelp from Plovac and then his hand was gone. Cole opened his eyes. Plovac had been tossed aside. His body was pinned to the far wall, his face exerting against some pressure only he could feel.

Kenny was off his gurney. Cole spotted him beating the shit out of Acne-scars. His fists pummeled the man's face as Acne-scars tried unsuccessfully to block the punches.

Plovac growled. Whatever was keeping him off balance had diminished.

You let them go, Cole. You fucking let them rip.

Jumping from the table, Cole tore toward he bastard while swinging the baton. The aide reached out toward him only to hear his fingers snap. Plovac cried out in shock and cradled his hand, his wailing now louder than the retreating wind.

"You've had it, kid." He lunged just as Cole swung. The nightstick smacked the man's jaw. Blood sprayed, decorating the tiles behind.

"Cole. Let's get the hell out of here." Kenny embraced him from behind and spoke in his ear.

Cole obeyed.

They fled the room, but not before spotting Slaver crouched in the corner, trying to be invisible. He was weeping like a child. Seeping blood mixed with his tears.

17

Kenny's First Lobotomy

WHEN COLE AND KENNY SCRAMMED from the shock treatment room, no one followed them. At least not yet. The two male aides had been beaten out of commission for the short term.

"Now's the time to run from this shitstorm. And I'm not talking about the weather," Kenny hissed as they ran down the hall and up the stairs to the first floor.

"Be careful. The secure ward's been damaged. The patients are loose." The pleasant nurse was by the main door peering outside. They nearly ran right into her. She stood there hugging herself even though the air was muggy. She wasn't the slightest bit fearful of them either, as far as Cole could tell. That made him feel good.

"What happened?" Kenny asked as he scanned the immediate area.

Cole couldn't believe what he was seeing. Cars were tossed all over the place like toys. Trees were stripped bare of leaves and pulled from the ground. Craning his neck, Cole was even more surprised to see that the area where they threw the football around was unscathed. Some branches were down in the surrounding woods beyond the playing field, but the trees were standing and healthy looking for the most part.

"Must've been a tornado," the nurse said. Her teeth chattered.

"You okay?" Cole asked her.

"I think so. It's probably shock."

As they stood there, Cole observed adult patients, all men, wandering around outside. Only some were dressed and they were all soaked. A couple of guys were fighting. Three guys were sprinting for the forest.

"You can't go out there," the nurse said. "They'll kill you. I swear to God."

"We'll take our chances," Kenny said. "We're screwed if we stay here. They'll never let us leave."

The nurse didn't argue. She only nodded. "I know. And I'm sorry."

"For what?" Cole asked.

She gazed at Cole. "For not helping you. They weren't treating you right."

"No big deal," Kenny replied. "Maybe you can throw them off the scent if they come looking for us."

Cole realized she was young, maybe around Peggy's age. "How come Peggy hasn't been back to work?"

Kenny, who looked like he was going to bolt at any second into the rain, paused and searched her face.

"She just hasn't. No one knows for sure. She might get fired for not showing up."

"Anyone talk to her?" Kenny asked.

"No. I mean, I don't think so. Not that I've heard."

"Shit." Kenny kicked the doorframe lightly. "C'mon, Cole. Now's as good a time as any." He pushed the crash bar on the door, which opened smoothly into the downpour. The wind had died down and the sky was a lighter gray. They inspected the grounds in both directions.

"Don't go out that way. Don't be damn fools."

Cole jumped around in surprise but Kenny just sighed. The voice was easily recognizable and friendly despite scaring the crap out of him.

Lambert eased his way from the lobby. "This place is a mess. Windows are missing and fences are down. A couple of men are dead back in one of the wards. An entire wall fell on them."

He strolled more casually than Cole would've expected under the circumstances. "My point is that those men who were killed were in the violent ward. The wall is down. The others are out there on the grounds and in the woods, desperate to get away."

"So are we," Kenny said, stretching to his fullest height. Cole thought he looked foolish—something he hadn't seen before in Kenny.

"Son, nine maniacs are on the run. If they find you, being killed would be the best part of your interaction with them. You don't want that."

"So, we should stay." This option clearly wasn't acceptable to Kenny. Cole didn't find it desirable either.

"I didn't say that. But there are other ways out," Lambert said with a grin.

Kenny beamed and slapped his forehead. "How could I forget?"

"That's right. Once you're out, follow the back trail. These clowns will be heading down to the valley toward town using the road. You can avoid them. There are cabins in the woods, too. Some folks might help ya."

Cole was nonplussed. "What other way out?"

Kenny grabbed Cole's arm and dragged him back down the stairs. "The tunnel. It goes in the other direction."

Cole stopped short and almost pulled Kenny off his feet. "Wait. The Dead Tunnel?'

"Yeah, c'mon, hurry. Those shitheads will be coming. And I'm talking about Plovac and the other cocksucker, not the crazy guys."

"Man, what happened here?"

After their sprint to the basement, they'd navigated to Daniel's office as quietly and quickly as possible. Cole was relieved that they didn't run into any of the other staff who had been in the shock treatment room when they made their escape. He and Kenny would be in big trouble after fighting with Plovac and the other guy.

There were shouts and wild laughter echoing off the walls. Neither could get a fix on their origin and location. Patients were still running free from the secure ward, and the staff had their hands full corralling them. Nobody was in the basement corridor at the moment, so it was fair sailing.

Things turned worse when they reached Daniel's office. The door was wide open. Papers, checklists, order forms, and tools were scattered all over.

Must've been a fight," Kenny said. "But who'd fight Daniel?"

"Someone wanting the keys to the tunnel?" Cole didn't add *like us*.

"Yeah, but. Still." Kenny was momentarily speechless.

"Is that blood?" Cole pointed to the floor and halfway up some hallway tiles on the wall. Splatters of red made a wild pattern of circles.

"Could be. Yeah, probably is." Kenny said. "If someone fought him for the keys to the tunnel, then he'd have them now. Let's check out the entrance. We're sitting ducks here." Kenny trotted silently in that direction without waiting for Cole. Cole took off at a run to catch up.

The collapsible gate had been unlocked and pushed aside. Once inside the gate, the floor changed from tile to concrete. Five additional steps brought them to the black door, which was about three inches ajar.

"I thought so," Kenny said. "Whoever fought with Daniel for the key went in already."

"Why'd he take the key with him?"

Kenny shrugged. "I don't know. Wait, yeah I do. The door at the other end is locked, too, probably. They'd need the key for that."

That made sense. But something else occurred to him. "Where's Daniel?"

Kenny pursed his lips.

"Good question. He might've gone for help."

Cole's attention turned to the concrete flooring. "Look. There's more blood." Actually, quite a bit more. Drops had turned into streaks. This didn't look good. "Do you think one of those violent crazy guys is in there?"

Kenny took a couple of steps into the tunnel. The overhead florescent lights were off, so he disappeared into the gloom in no time. His footsteps stopped after a few paces.

Kenny came back into view. "It's dead quiet down there. Whoever it was is probably long gone."

Cole wasn't reassured, but they'd come this far. What

else could they do? He inspected the wall outside the door, looking for the light switch he'd seen Daniel use.

There. He flicked the switch. Nothing happened. Flipping the switch frantically a few more times didn't change anything. The lights in the tunnel weren't working.

Kenny groaned. "Shit. You gotta be kidding."

"It's so dark in there. Can we make it?" Cole's voice was high-pitched and shaky.

"You saw it when Daniel showed us. The floor was flat. We can do it. We just need to go slow."

Cole was uneasy. Being in a pitch-black tunnel—the Dead Tunnel, no less—and trying to find their way when there could be a disturbed killer down there...

"I think I saw a flashlight in Daniel's office," Cole announced.

Kenny's face brightened. "That's right. I did, too. On the desk. Wait here." Kenny sprinted away before Cole could say anything to stop him.

The silence in the tunnel only added to his fear. Elsewhere, both down the hall and above his head, Cole could hear voices. He couldn't make out the words, but the sense of urgency was unmistakable. Patients needed to be corralled soon and order had to be restored. Two of the male staff were likely chomping at the bit to hunt down Kenny and him, but for the moment maybe they'd been cornered into helping with the larger task of bringing the asylum under control. This could buy them time.

Kenny materialized out of nowhere, panting slightly. "Couldn't find it right away." He held up the flashlight triumphantly.

Cole nodded, satisfied. At least this was something.

Kenny pushed the switch to turn on the flashlight. A weak

beam shot out. Cole couldn't believe it. The battery was on its last legs. Who knew if it would stay lit for the entire journey?

"Shit," Kenny muttered under his breath. "Let's keep it off for as long as possible and then turn it on for a few seconds at a time.

That defeated the purpose, but they had no other options.

"Let's go." Kenny walked into the darkness. Cole followed.

There was enough light from the basement hallway to guide them for longer than Cole would've expected. Kenny crept along slowly, placing one foot in front of the other gingerly. Cole found the entire thing unnerving despite Kenny's bravado.

The indirect light from the hallway behind them was diminishing rapidly. Kenny stopped walking. "I'll turn it on now."

Cole nodded his assent, even though Kenny couldn't see it.

The muffled sound of Kenny's hand fiddling with the flashlight was swift. He shifted slightly, and the amber glow shot toward the ceiling.

Kenny smiled, looking demonic with the light under his face, and then he crashed backward to the floor. His surprised cry was short and followed by another curse.

"Kenny?" Cole squealed. The flashlight rocked on the floor. The swaying light dimly illuminated the scene. The older boy was trying to lift himself up on his elbows.

He had fallen over a person crumpled on the ground—at least Cole thought it was a person. Arms and legs were splayed in all directions. Remnants of a face hidden by shadows were barely visible.

"Oh, damn." Kenny scrambled to his feet. His pants and T-shirt had smears of blood on them.

"Who is it?" Cole's voice nearly pitched into panic.

Kenny retrieved the flashlight and shone it in the body's face. Cole still wasn't sure if it *was* a person. Where there should have been eyes and a nose was nothing but a bloody pulp. Chunks of white shards that had to be bone were poking out of coin-sized pools of blood and slime gathering in shattered remains.

"Oh, man. That's Daniel."

Cole shuddered. "How can you tell? His face is smashed."

Kenny shifted the light. "The uniform."

Yes, there it was. Daniel's typical getup complete with his name embroidered on his shirt.

"What do we do?"

Kenny didn't hesitate. "Keep going. There's nothing we can do for him. C'mon." He resumed his trek, pointing the faint beam of light in front of him. Once again, Cole ran to catch up.

Daniel had been beaten to a pulp by somebody. It had to be one of the crazy men from the secure ward. Could he have done it with his fists? An object was more likely. Something like a hammer or baseball bat.

A larger concern occurred to Cole. Where was the person who did this? Kenny thought he was long gone. God, he hoped so.

Cole was relieved to see that Kenny wasn't taking anything for granted. Kenny moved slowly, with Cole following less than an arm's length behind. The flashlight was only turned on for a few seconds at a time, and only when Kenny crouched down. It would look disorienting to anyone trying to keep track of their progress. The rest of their advance was conducted flush with the wall on the right-hand side of the tunnel.

A girl started crying.

Cole gasped and flung out his hand to catch Kenny's shoulder.

"What?" Kenny hissed.

"Do you hear that?"

"No. Hear what?"

"Oh, man." Cole kept his voice low.

The flashlight beam reappeared. Kenny made a brief sweep, catching nothing. The light shut off. Kenny, thankfully, said nothing. He stood, waiting for Cole.

For his part, Cole knew what was happening. Only he could hear the crying—and only he could see the shapes that were materializing. Cole thought of flames on a candle. Long, stretched flames. Except these were person-sized. One appeared right next to where they were standing. Then another just a few feet away. Then another and another, each one farther down the tunnel.

"You don't see the things?"

"No. Let's keep going."

"Wait."

The flames weren't yellow like a candle flame, but white. As Cole watched, the flames transformed into figures standing perfectly straight, like soldiers at inspection. Except they were crying. All of them, not just the one girl.

Like the white flames they'd been, the figures glowed in the dark. Some were roughly his age, some were teenagers like Kenny, some seemed a little older than that. Both boys and girls. And they weren't wearing any clothes.

The sobs became screams.

Crap, not this again. Cole winced and covered his ears.

The screamers remained immobile in their upright posture. Their eyes reflected pure horror as they watched the approach of someone coming from the asylum. Cole turned his head sharply and almost fell in the process. He felt Kenny's hand steadying him.

"What're you seeing?"

Cole ignored him only because he didn't see anything coming from where they just came. He wanted to say *Let's keep going* but he had no words.

The scream of the girl standing closest to him intensified. Her fear was nearly tangible. When her stomach split open just below her rib cage and continued to her crotch, Cole involuntarily jumped back. His head slammed into the wall but his pain didn't register.

The split was pulled apart by unseen hands, and her guts spilled out to the floor. Cole gagged and closed his eyes. When he opened them, he shifted his attention farther down the line. The same thing happened to a boy. Another boy's face was slit at his hairline. The invisible hand clasped on to the lower slit and yanked. The skin of the boy's face was stripped from his head. His scream was unbearable. And still, the figures stood perfectly straight with their hands at their sides.

"Go, go," Cole cried. "We need to go."

Kenny didn't question. He reached back, took hold of Cole's hand, and pulled him along. They continued hugging the wall, Cole trying to focus straight ahead or at the ground. He couldn't bear to watch the kids getting ripped to pieces. The screams turned into wails as the figures endured the ever-lasting pain of their torture.

There was a vague trace of light in front of them. They had to be getting closer to the end, didn't they? The uproar of terror continued unabated, but seemed more distant somehow. Cole wondered if maybe he was getting used to it.

With no warning, Kenny sprang to his right and collided

with something metallic. Cole was yanked in the same direction until Kenny let go of his hand. He slammed into a jutting corner and fell in the same direction as Kenny.

"Ow, damn," Kenny said, gritting his teeth. He was on the ground, lying downhill. Cole was on Kenny's legs. Making things worse, it was pitch black.

"What happened?" Cole's shoulder smarted.

"I forgot about these," Kenny said.

Then Cole remembered. There were indentations in the walls that led to rooms or storage spaces. They'd fallen into one. The metal clanging sound was Kenny's head as he hit the door. The door opened easily and Kenny kept falling. There were two steps leading down into the room, which Kenny was now lying on.

Kenny got to his feet after Cole shuffled off his legs. He stepped into the room while holding the door open. "I dropped the flashlight in here. I can't believe it turned off. We're fucked if it's broken."

Cole sighed. He stuck his head back out into the tunnel. The latest set of screaming ghosts were gone. The tunnel was vacant. And pitch black again. The hint of light he thought he saw before was only wishful thinking. As he withdrew his head, there was a faint noise, like a tap.

Cole froze.

Was someone following them? A real someone and not a ghost? Straining, Cole tried to clear his mind and listen. Nothing. It had to be his imagination or a rat or a water drip. Yeah, dripping water. With all the rain from the storm, water would be seeping in from outside.

Reluctantly, Cole edged back into the room off the tunnel. Even as his eyes adjusted, the room remained completely dark.

Cole heard Kenny making some weird slapping noises on the floor.

"What're you doing?"

"Looking for the flashlight. I told you," Kenny said. "Get your ass down here and help me."

Cole squatted carefully so as not to pitch himself onto something dangerous. He swatted and patted his palms blindly on the floor. All he felt was dust and dirt, but he kept going while widely expanding the arc of his search.

After an interminable length of time, Cole heard a clicki-ty-click sound to his right.

"Found it." Kenny's disembodied voice floated in the darkness. More patting sounds ensued. "Well, shit. I hit it and it rolled away." More patting. "Wait, here."

A muted ray of light chased the darkness, but not by much. Murky shadows loomed over the two of them sprawled on the floor. Old crates randomly rested in the gloom. Saw-horses were positioned along the far wall as if ready for something to rest across them.

Like a coffin.

"We're in the makeshift morgue," Kenny said.

"Yeah, gosh."

"There's gotta be a light in here." Kenny's flashlight flitted along the walls. It stopped right next to the door.

Cole could barely make out the old-fashioned light switch. Two buttons. Press one for on, the other for off. Cole made his way over since he was closer. He pushed the extended button. Nothing happened. He tried a few more times, alternating buttons even though he knew it was fruitless.

"Just great. None of the lights work." Kenny flashed the beam around.

Located on the opposite wall from the entrance stood another door.

"Where does that go?" Cole asked. He took a breath and wasn't surprised when it shuddered all the way in.

"Damned if I know." Kenny replied, keeping his voice low. He walked slowly toward the door, all the while sweeping the light. More crates, sawhorses with wooden planks lying across them, and a table came into view.

Kenny altered his course slightly to check out the table. Cole peered around him. There were all kinds of tools, and—this really creeped him out—knives of different sizes. He saw some jars, picked up a couple, and held them under Kenny's light.

"Alum. What's that?"

Kenny shook his head.

Cole continued his inspection. "Another alum. Pickling salt." Cole looked at Kenny. "What're these for?"

"Beats me."

Cole returned the jars and spotted a plastic bottle. He recognized this one. Liquid dish soap.

These items held no interest for Kenny. He was running his hand across the tools. He picked up a screwdriver and hammer and placed them in his pockets. "Maybe we'll need them," he said. The walk to the other door resumed.

There was a tap behind them.

They both spun, but Kenny was quicker. The beam hit Cole square in the eyes, blinding him. He crouched down instinctively. Kenny grabbed him and swung him to the side. It took only moments for Cole to see again. He stood, and Kenny's arm remained over his shoulder. The flashlight darted across the entire room, revealing nothing.

Cole exhaled. He hadn't realized he was holding his breath.

"Did we leave the door open?" Kenny played with the light on the door, which was open a couple of inches.

"No. I'm pretty, um...I don't know." Cole thought he'd sink into the floor,

"Shit. Well, let's close it." Kenny strode to the door and shut the door softly. On his way back to Cole, he checked from side to side again.

"This is stupid." Kenny resumed his march to the closed door at the far side of the room. It opened with a screech. Cole walked to Kenny's side and peered into the room from the entrance.

In a far corner stood an old freezer. Cole looked around and found another freezer. Boards leaned against the wall with stretched-out clothes hanging from hooks or pins.

Then Cole was shoved violently into the room. Kenny followed, falling on top of him.

Cole's anxiety soared. When Kenny's body began thumping his own, Cole knew Kenny was being kicked. He could make out the sounds of swiftly shifting feet.

"Well, well, hello, boys."

Kenny's weight lifted, and Cole rolled over in time to see Plovac rain down punches on Kenny's face and head. Kenny's arms flailed to block the fists and succeeded only in deflecting one or two. After a few additional blows, he dropped Kenny.

Cole tried to scramble backward like a crab. In two strides, Plovac was on him and delivered a kick to his groin. Cole collapsed in a ball and couldn't defend himself when Plovac picked him up and tossed him roughly into the upright freezer. The impact was paralyzing, and Cole landed with a helpless groan. Above him, the handle on the freezer had been jarred enough to loosen and then release—which allowed the lid to spring open.

"Payback time, you little shits. Think you're men enough to take me on? Let's see it." The aide stood on spread legs with his arms folded. He didn't even sound winded.

This was going to be trouble. Every inch of Cole's body throbbed in agony, but even in perfect condition, he couldn't take on Plovac. He'd need Kenny. And Kenny was having his own problems. Cole glanced over and saw Kenny struggling to get upright.

Cole chanced a second look at the aide. Shadows ran across Plovac's face as he turned his head in all directions to take in the room. One side of his jaw was swollen from when Cole clobbered him with the nightstick.

"What in *the* hell is this place? Hoo-wee, you boys found us an interesting site for our get-together."

Despite his pain, Cole couldn't help following the bastard's eyes. He had already noticed the large wooden boards leaning against a wall and the clothes stretched out on them. Except they weren't clothes.

They were hides in the process of tanning.

The hides were human.

On the other side of the room, hides for which the preparation work had been completed hung on hangers and were strung along a rope clothesline.

Plovac's breathing picked up. At first Cole thought he was frightened, but no, he sounded excited. The man reached for the flashlight and slapped it against his palm.

"Shit. Needs batteries." Plovac marched to the freezer and Cole instinctually covered his balls. Plovac ignored him as he shined the light into the freezer.

"God fucking damn. That's where she went." He stepped back and chuckled. "Man, who did this shit?"

Cole kept his eyes on Plovac and gasped when Kenny lunged out of the darkness and jumped onto his back. Plovac twisted slightly, but Kenny had his left arm around his throat in an instant.

Kenny's right arm extended over his head. The amber glow from the flashlight was enough to illuminate the screwdriver in Kenny's hand—the very screwdriver he'd pocketed moments before on a hunch. It paused momentarily at the top of the arc before his arm descended in a blur. The shank plunged easily into Plovac's right eye, all the way to the handle.

Plovac wavered but remained standing. Kenny dropped to the floor, rolled twice, and jumped back up.

Cole was sitting practically at Plovac's feet. Liquid dripped from the man's face, and Cole felt the wetness on his arm.

"Ugh." He scooted sideways along the freezer.

Plovac dropped the flashlight. It clattered to the floor but astoundingly remained lit.

"Grab it," Kenny said.

Cole did, and just in time.

Plovac fell to his knees and then face first into the freezer. His descent jostled the handle of the screwdriver, which sliced up more of his brain.

Even though it was sick, Cole couldn't help himself. "Kenny, you performed your first lobotomy."

Plovac crumpled to the floor.

18

The ECT Review

"LIKE OTHER HOSPITALS IN THE early- to mid-twentieth century, there wasn't much in terms of treatment options. Maybe I should say good treatment options. Psychiatric care was in its infancy."

Regardless of who led the tour, this was the opening gambit for the basement.

"Early on, things like hydrotherapy, ice baths, insulin-shock therapy, and frontal lobotomies were conducted. All of these are now recognized as cruel and brutal. In all likelihood, they were often used as a way to punish unruly patients.

"Then there was ECT, or electroconvulsive therapy. My understanding is that ECT is still used today, but the procedures are more sophisticated and better understood. Back then, a lot was left to chance. For instance, early on, they didn't use muscle relaxants or anesthesia. The convulsions suffered by patients were often severe enough that they broke bones and chipped teeth."

Chaz let that information settle for a bit. Too much lecturing on tours could be deadly, so they wanted to avoid excessive speeches. The basement corridor also had a more confined feeling to it compared to the upper floors. People became uneasy, and it was smart to keep folks moving.

"Using ECT with kids started in the nineteen forties and fifties. It became controversial at some point—still is, although according to the stuff Evie and I found, it looks like ECT is now seen as okay for some kids. We're not doctors, so don't rely on our interpretation."

The group smiled.

Evie offered Chaz a short respite. "ECT was used here with kids and adults. However, until the nineteen seventies, it was sometimes used for the wrong reasons. Chaz talked about punishment before. The patients here who acted out for too long often got shocked. And for the boys, if they were suspected of being homosexual, they were given shocks to help cure their sexual orientation."

The Beard's wife raised her hand. "So, the kids who came out were shocked? Why would they disclose under these circumstances?"

Evie shook her head. "They didn't. It was too dangerous."

"How did they suspect, then, that a kid might be gay?" One of the college girls.

Evie looked to Chaz, who took over. Tag-teaming was working well. "Evidently, there was a belief in the hospital that masturbation caused homosexuality. So if a boy, or man for that matter, was caught doing that, they were zapped."

"Eew," said the girl.

The oldest kid also scrunched up his nose.

"The lore was passed down year after year that you could get shocked if, you know, they caught you red-handed."

The crowd groaned. Mom didn't find it very funny, but her husband smiled.

"Let's take a look at the ECT room."

Evie led the group a few paces down the hall and opened a door stenciled with the words "Treatment Room." From the outside, it was nothing to write home about, but inside was a different story. The first time Chaz saw it he was shocked by how big it was. Teams of five or six people could fit in here easily. A standard-looking examination table stood near the center of the room, covered with fake green leather upholstery. Chaz didn't notice the straps dangling from the sides until a few seconds later. He'd known people had been strapped down, but actually seeing the entire row of four straps was something else. Thanks to scenes from movies, he could visualize people struggling against them as electric current cruised through their brains.

Behind the table was the ECT machine. Unlike the room, this item was smaller than he'd expected. The electrodes looked like an ancient, and cheap, set of headphones.

Other than the table (which may not have been original to the room) and the ECT machine (which was, Chaz later learned), there was nothing else. Only after seeing a documentary showing ECT in action did Chaz realize that the extra space was for the roomful of people needed to help prepare the patient.

The crowd floated around the room, getting a feel for the space and examining the machine. Chaz often wondered how people felt about the equipment, but they rarely said anything.

"The machine is unplugged, by the way," Evie said to the

oldest kid, who'd extended a hand out toward the headgear. "It's okay, you can touch it."

"We bring people into this room to tell one of the strangest stories to come out of Saint Edwards," Chaz began. "It involves a patient who was about ten or twelve when he arrived here, probably in the fifties or sixties. In hospital folklore he was referred to as Twilight Eyes. He was only here a short time, but he evidently made quite an impact.

"His arrival caused an immediate uproar. Not among the patients, but the wildlife in the area. From his first day, birds would flock in unusual patterns, and deer would step out of the woods just to watch for him. Day and night this would happen. This apparently freaked out the patients, and probably the staff, too."

As always, he paused at this point to let the suspense build.

"Here's where it gets a little bizarre. Supposedly this boy had psychic powers of some sort. The patients evidently caught on to this. Within days, the supervising doctor felt that electric shock therapy was just what they needed to set the young man on the right path."

"So even the doctors were scared of him," said one of the kids. "Like they wanted to get back at him or something."

"That's right," Evie answered.

Chaz waited a beat for any other comments, then continued. "The boy was taken down here and strapped to that table for his ECT." Chaz motioned in the table's direction. The straps, which had looked harmless moments before, now took on a sinister cast. "Twilight Eyes knew what was coming—he had psychic powers after all—and he was really upset. He carried on and became combative. Until they got the straps in place, Twilight Eyes kept kicking, punching, and screaming. It took a lot of people to hold him down and strap him in.

"Here's the creepy part. Keep in mind that this story was gleaned from multiple accounts of people who were in the room, like nurses and staff. This kid's screaming and they're trying to get the IV meds going when suddenly he really explodes. Somehow he gets a leg free and kicks a nurse. Then, out of the blue, the window shatters. Instruments start flying around the room. Adults are knocked off their feet."

Chaz took a breath. Everyone was silent. He could hear a pin drop.

"Right at that moment, a shadow of some sort—in human form—materializes in the room. The figure shouts, 'Leave the boy alone,' and throws itself on top of the boy to protect him. The room is in chaos. People are panicking. Some are injured. But in the end, they unstrap Twilight Eyes and let him go. He doesn't receive the shock treatment."

"Cool," said the oldest kid. His little brother nodded vigorously in agreement.

"Meantime, the rest of the asylum heard the uproar and went ballistic. It was like a revolt. Staff members were assaulted and a number of men escaped. They were all rounded up quickly by law enforcement, though. This location is fairly isolated, and back then it was even more so. Not many places to hide."

Silence from the group.

Finally, Potbelly broke it. "And?"

Chaz expected this but still played along according to the script. "And, what?"

"What happened to Twilight Eyes?"

"Ah. I hate to say it, but we don't know. Supposedly he was moved to a different institution, but there's no record of this. I mean, there probably is, but we don't know his real name to check." This part was true. Both Chaz and Evie had scoured Saint Edwards records, looking for some kind of account similar to Twilight Eyes. They weren't successful.

"Did he get the shock treatment later on?"

"We don't know that either. But I sure wouldn't give it to him after that happened, would you?"

The group, like many others before them, was quiet after this presentation, thinking about the story. They'd also been on their feet for about an hour.

"Shall we move on to our last stop?"

After the mutterings of assent, they walked farther down the hall and came to a doorway that was covered by a collapsible gate. For reasons of liability, although Chaz couldn't imagine what those could be, they wouldn't be able to open the gate and go through. It was too bad, because this locale was especially eerie.

"Ladies and gentlemen, you are looking at the Dead Tunnel."

The energy level picked up as individuals peered through the gate to stare down the tunnel. Their efforts were futile, as it was completely dark.

"There's a doorway beyond the gate. That door is open now. The tunnel itself goes underground for quite a ways. Maybe fifty to seventy-five yards. It's sealed at the other end, so we can't go out that way. But you used to be able to."

"Why's it called the Dead Tunnel?" said Dad.

"Yes, they called it the Dead Tunnel because that was the way they used to take out dead bodies without freaking out the other patients. The corpses could be wheeled down the tunnel, and they'd meet up with an ambulance to take them to town. Or, if the patient was destitute, they would be buried out back."

Chaz took this opportunity to flick the switch on the wall. Florescent lights burst into action. There were a few exclamations of surprise, but Chaz always thought the display was anticlimactic. What you saw was...a tunnel. Nothing else. Certainly not ghosts or supernatural beings.

"There's a sinister history here, though, of a decidedly human nature. At some point, a patient killed two staff members down here. Midway down the tunnel, right after the curve you see ahead, there's a small room. It might've been a fallout shelter back in the sixties. Either way, it served as a makeshift morgue. Sometimes when people died here, the authorities couldn't always get here right away to collect them."

"Did that many people die here?" one of the wives said.

"Remember, for a short time this was a sanatorium, and there were tuberculosis patients. Some of those certainly died. And when it was an asylum, there were probably also deaths. People committed suicide, they were frail, some had been here for decades. Patients were probably murdered, too. You can see that happening easily enough."

Two people looked at their watches. Some eyes wandered. Only the old dude looked focused. He stared unblinking down the tunnel.

"Shall we go upstairs?"

19

The Dead Tunnel

THE TWO OF THEM REMAINED stationary for who knew how long. Plovac hadn't moved from his position on the floor. Cole was conscious of trying to catch his breath and waiting for his pain to subside. Kenny still stood, but he was wavering some. Cole figured he had to be hurting too.

When Kenny finally moved, it was to retrieve the flashlight and check out the open freezer.

"Holy shit."

Cole pushed off the floor and stood unsteadily. He felt woozy and a little nauseous. Still, he had to see what caused Kenny and Plovac to react the way they did.

He regretted it immediately. His nausea increased by leaps and bounds.

Nurse Peggy was in the freezer. And not all in one piece, either.

She had been hacked apart. Arms and legs were at the bottom and her torso was on top. He only knew it was

Peggy because her head, perched in the corner, was looking skyward.

Cole speedily rotated so his back was to the freezer. The motion added to his nausea and he started retching. His stomach was empty, so nothing came up except drool. He slid down the freezer to sit on the floor.

Kenny joined him. A couple of times he started to say something but quit each time. He settled for clearing his throat.

In the short time he'd known Kenny, Cole had never seen him unable to speak.

Finally: "And they think we're crazy."

There was nothing for Cole to say. He focus gradually turned to the room. Kenny fiddled with the light. It danced around, making it impossible to concentrate on the items scattered about.

Then it hit him. The hides. Drying on the boards. They looked human.

Oh God.

Cole stood, his nausea forgotten. "Kenny." He reached for Kenny's arm, trying to pull him up.

"What?" A cautious whisper.

Dear God, it couldn't be.

"Kenny." A sense of shock and urgency engulfed him. "Kenny." Almost a cry.

"What, Cole? Damn." A sharp intake of air as Kenny looked up. "Sweet Jesus."

Cole swiped the light from Kenny and walked to the boards.

They *were* human hides. Parts of them anyway.

Oh no. No. No. No.

The first was a boy. Arms and feet were missing. But the

rest of him was drying on the board. The skin from the chest and torso had been sectioned and spread out. Maybe four or five pieces in all. Cole didn't count. The same for the legs and pelvis area. The head and face had been split like an orange peel so it could flatten. But the identity was unmistakable.

The second was a girl. This time the arms and legs had been discarded. She too had been sliced into sections. Maybe six pieces in all. Her head and face torn in the same manner as the boy.

Oh my God.

Cole's teeth chattered. His mind couldn't fully grasp the insanity of the tanner. The boy and girl had been skinned and fleshed—he remembered that second term from somewhere, it was where their guts had been cleaned out. Then they had been cleaned and left to dry. The actual tanning would be completed sometime soon.

Skinned and fleshed.

Behind him, Kenny groaned.

In front of him, his friends Timmy and Cynthia stared hauntingly from the board. Cynthia's self-administered cuts to her face were still visible.

Cole took a long backward step. Kenny, a second behind, did the same.

Simon says take one giant step back.

The ridiculous thought came unbidden to Cole's mind.

The flashlight trembled in his hand. The beam quivered. Kenny lunged to grab it from him before it fell to the floor.

He squeezed his eyes shut. Causes and explanations for all they'd seen were beyond comprehension. And this wasn't even counting Plovac's appearance and ultimate demise. There was only one idea that Cole could entertain.

"We need to get outta here."

"Yeah."

Still they didn't move. Couldn't move, really. Kids that they knew, and Nurse Peggy, had been crushed and torn, their bodies defiled in the most evil way possible. All within a few days...

The scope of the horror was beyond Cole's ability to understand.

From behind, a faint rubbing noise meshed with the haunting silence of the room. The sound was soft, but not random. There was purpose behind the movement.

The hairs on the back of Cole's head tingled. He couldn't tell why it unnerved him because it was a familiar sound. A nonthreatening sound. He just couldn't place it.

Kenny heard it too. He turned toward Cole slowly. Cole did the same until they were facing each other. Kenny's eyes, barely visible in the shadows thrown by the flashlight, merely looked puzzled. Cole suspected his eyes reflected sheer terror.

They continued their rotation until they faced the direction of the sound.

The completed hides on hangers. Human hides suspended on a clothesline, displayed like they'd be in a closet in a bedroom. They swayed in a room with no breeze. There was a space between two groups of hides that hadn't been there before.

Yes, Cole realized, that was the sound. The normal everyday sound of hangers being pushed along the rope of a clothesline. A safe sound.

Except when it wasn't.

Like now.

The gap between the hides was ink black. No light penetrated the shadows.

But something was there. A sense of presence caused by a

miniscule shift in space. Dust particles may have reflected the dim light or the hint of an exhale. Something making itself known. They only had to wait.

Cole reached out to Kenny's left arm. He was shaking so hard that he didn't think he could grasp it.

The flashlight in Kenny's right hand slowly rose. The beam crossed the floor, barely dispelling the darkness. When the light reached the space, the murkiness seemed to overpower it. Yet there it was. A figure stood ramrod straight. Menacing. Unforgiving.

"What the hell?" Kenny whispered.

The figure stepped forward, ducking under the clothesline, then straightening. The stuff of nightmares.

Its face was distorted, covered with a mask that concealed its entire head—almost like a hood. Attached to this were scraps of hides.

My God, it's wearing the hides of other kids.

There were cheeks and ears. A flattened nose. Each safety-pinned, *yes, safety-pinned*, to the mask.

Cole now saw that the mask was a burlap sack. Eyeholes had been cut. Inside the holes, barely visible eyeballs darted across the scene.

Garments comprised of loosely stitched hides draped its shoulders. A belt around its waist allowed the figure to drape sections of hides from the lower halves of former victims.

The Creeper.

"Here." Kenny shoved the flashlight into Cole's hands. "Get your ass outta here."

Kenny charged the Creeper, heedless of any danger. His fists were clenched, ready to strike. The Creeper's arm lifted with a flailing motion when Kenny was nearly at striking distance. Unexpectedly, Kenny stopped in his tracks, seemingly caught off guard.

Why'd you stop? No, Kenny!

But then he saw. As did Kenny, who looked down at his side.

Kenny's pants and T-shirt had been sliced. As if canal locks had been opened, blood seeped through the material, darkening it at a dramatic rate.

Kenny looked up with a baffled expression, as if he was going to ask what happened.

The Creeper also stood as if waiting. It raised a hand above its head, holding a knife high. Before Cole could shout a warning, the arm descended. The Creeper's wrist struck Kenny's head a glancing blow, knocking its trajectory angle off course. The knife sliced Kenny's shoulder and clattered to the floor.

It missed. How…?

It was having trouble seeing with the eyeholes. Had to be.

"Kenny!"

"Go!"

Instead, Cole ran for the knife, crouching down as he approached.

The Creeper's bare foot—

Not a monster but a man—

kicked the knife out of reach.

"Dammit." Cole clawed along the floor, trying to locate the knife. The beam of light danced dizzyingly through the room.

"Cole, go!"

Kenny's voice was muffled. Cole glanced up to watch the Creeper grab the older boy's head in both of his hands and slam it brutally against a wall. Kenny slumped lifelessly to the floor.

There was only one course of action now. Cole scrambled for the door to the next room. His legs were like gelatin, slipping and kicking awkwardly. He reached for the doorframe and seized it in an effort to pull himself through.

One step into the next room.

Yes!

The Creeper clutched his other leg. Cole pulled, screaming at the same time—only to fall face first on the concrete floor. His nose and chin flared with white pain.

The Creeper was upon him, grabbing his hips and turning him onto his back in a single motion.

Just like the other night in bed.

Cole inhaled and swung his fists, thrashing in all directions. He screamed again until he was out of breath and his vocal cords produced only a croak.

The Creeper slapped him once, paused momentarily, and then a second time.

"There." The thing sat on his legs.

Cole felt an icy hand slip under his T-shirt.

"You'll do nicely," the voice rasped. "Young and tender."

The head leaned closer. Eyes peered through the slots in the burlap. "I've been waiting for this moment."

Cole didn't know what he was doing. His flailing arms had stopped without his noticing. He stared upward at the burlap sack and the pieces of hide from long-dead kids dangling in his face.

Without any forethought, he snatched the burlap sack and yanked. It came off easily. He threw it forcefully above and beyond him. And gawked at the face that had been hidden under the burlap.

"Dale?"

Dale glared, rage building behind his eyes. Both of the man's fists appeared in Cole's vision for a moment, and then they began pummeling. Cole cried out but was cut off when Dale's hands clasped around his neck and squeezed harder than Cole thought possible.

Streaks of light sparkled and burst in his vision. Cole slapped at the man's arms helplessly. His grip didn't budge.

I'm dying.

A burst of light this time. Then a loud pop. Additional bursts followed by pops. Something had burst in his brain for sure.

Dale's forehead and scalp exploded. Blood splashed everywhere.

My blood? No...

Dale's hands mercifully released.

Air entered Cole's lungs, seemingly of its own volition.

Shouts.

The crackle of a walkie-talkie.

Running. More voices. Lights. Bright lights.

Hands grasped Dale and rolled him to the side. Gunk from the top of his head, which Cole saw was now gone, spilled out.

Roy, dressed in his hospital garb, had a badge clipped to the waist of his pants. Roy lifted his shirt and placed a revolver in a shoulder holster. He pulled the shirt down to cover the gun and holster. He leaned over Cole and looked into his eyes.

"Can you breathe?"

Cole nodded. He didn't think he could talk, though.

"Can you move?"

Cole tested his arms and legs. Then his head. He could move them all, but his neck hurt.

"Here, sit up."

Cole sat up slowly. Everything seemed to work, but the pain was like electric jolts to every part of his body.

People were coming into the room in droves. Some were stepping over him into the other room. There were curses and gasps when they saw what it contained. Urgent voices seemed to be coming from where Kenny had fallen.

"Okay, Nurse, can you check him out?"

Cole looked up and saw Nurse Stern coming closer. Her skin was as white as her uniform. Good.

He turned back to Roy and saw the badge again. He looked into the man's face.

"I told you I wasn't a nurse."

Cole sat on the concrete floor of the Dead Tunnel. His back was propped against the wall, and he could see the exit about twenty yards away. The weather had turned sunny, but he had no idea what time it was. He hadn't eaten since forever, but he wasn't hungry yet. Although Nurse Stern had talked about a milkshake, which made him think he could get hungry at any moment.

The plan was to take him to the hospital in town to get checked out as a precaution. Nurse Stern had given him the once-over and said he'd probably be okay, but she wanted to make sure. Throat injuries could be sneaky and serious. The hospital could check more thoroughly than she could. At the very least, it could take a few days or even a week for swelling and bruising to subside. That meant a sore throat and difficulty talking for the time being.

Kenny was taken out on a stretcher, so he was alive at least. Cole felt good about that but was still worried. Maybe he'd get a chance to see him at the hospital. The two dirtbags in the rooms off the tunnel were dead as doornails, according to a cop. But Cole already knew that.

The asylum had taken a direct hit from a tornado. Lots of damage, evidently. Not that Cole cared. Some patients were hurt and killed. Same with a few staff. The ambulances were taking the seriously hurt people into town first. Cole was far back in that line. This, he was thankful for.

All different kinds of police had shown up. Everyone was falling over each other to check out the sights in the back room. No need to worry about catching the bad guy, since he'd had his head blown off. Now they were trying to figure out if Plovac had been in on the massacres with Dale. Cole figured he wasn't since he was surprised to find Peggy. But who knew? Besides, no one asked him, so he kept his ideas to himself.

Roy and then some other bigwig cop asked him about Dale. Even with his throat killing him, Cole told them what happened. Everybody believed him, which was a unique experience. Typically no one ever did.

Part of him was tempted to get up and walk out of the tunnel and keep going. The thought had occurred to him multiple times.

"Probably not a good idea." Lambert's voice. Cole could tell without turning to look. When he did, the muscles in his neck protested a little. Nurse Stern said that could get worse before it got better.

"Hi." It came out raspy.

The old man sat beside him away from the tunnel exit. The effort was not smooth and involved a lot of groaning.

"Boy, how can you find this comfortable?"

Cole shrugged but smiled a little.

"Hurts to talk?"

Cole nodded and tried "Yeah." He sounded like a frog.

Lambert produced a short round of his rumbling laughter.

"Quite a morning, huh? This gonna go down in Saint Edwards lore for sure. They'll talk about it for ages."

"Kenny." Cole whispered. He found that whispering didn't hurt as bad.

"You're worried about him. I know. He'll be fine, though."

Cole stared, wanting to believe. "How d'ya know?" He stuck with the whisper.

Lambert chuckled again. "I'm a seer."

Cole smiled. And believed. "I forgot."

"I know you did."

"Did you know?" The whispering strategy was starting to fail. Pain was building with the effort.

"That Dale was the Creeper?"

Cole nodded.

"No idea. I didn't pick that one up. I can't see everything. You're stronger than me, I think. Did you see it?"

Cole thought that he *should've*. He'd seen the Creeper a couple of times, both when Dale was the only one on duty— and hadn't been around. Now that he thought back on it, he should've put two and two together.

"You was scared outta your mind, son. There's no way you coulda known that thing was Dale. In the dark and in a strange place."

Cole considered this. He would've liked to think Lambert was right. He'd feel less guilty.

"Besides. He's been at this for years and years. And nobody

official here caught him. How do you expect a brand new kid to figure it out? Nope. Not your fault."

Lambert gazed up and down the tunnel for a few seconds. "Funny how the police had some kind of idea. They had that cop undercover."

That was fortunate. Roy had been looking furiously for both him and Kenny and traced them to the tunnel. He found poor Daniel, who was probably killed by Dale after the struggle for the tunnel keys. The maintenance man must've chased Dale down in the tunnel where he met his end. Cole's screams as he tried to escape Dale's clutches brought Roy to his rescue. Yes, Roy's being there was fortunate. Too bad he wasn't early enough to save Timmy and Cynthia.

"From what I learned," Lambert said, "Dale volunteered to arrange for your two friends to be picked up by the coroner's office. Except he didn't. You follow what I'm saying, Cole?"

Cole found his mind careening down dark, twisted passageways. He sure didn't want to ever get lost in any of them. "Do you mean he tricked the whole asylum into thinking he was gonna take care of their bodies? Get them to where they were supposed to go?"

"Apparently so. Instead he snuck their bodies down here last night. He worked the entire night, preparing them. Work of the devil." Lambert spat disgustedly. "The damn things adults do to kids."

"I bet Peggy was suspicious of him," Cole said. "That got her killed."

"Hmm. Hadn't thought about that. I figured Dale was tired of Peggy messing with one of *his* kids."

Cole looked fiercely at Lambert. "You think he knew? Oh wait. You're a seer."

Lambert smiled wistfully. "No, that's just a guess on my part. Yours is as good as mine."

They sat quietly for a few minutes. Cole's pain was intensifying and his muscles were getting stiff.

"Here comes the battle-axe." Lambert nodded in the direction of an approaching Nurse Stern. "I should go."

Lambert stood easier than he'd sat minutes ago. He winked at Cole and strolled in Nurse Stern's direction.

"See ya, Lambert," Cole squawked.

Nurse Stern's steps faltered for a moment. Then she regained her stride and walked over.

"Cole, I'll take you to the main entrance. Officer Roy will drive you to the hospital."

"Okay." Cole felt a small surge of joy. He couldn't help liking the guy since he'd saved Cole's life.

They walked side by side and passed by the indentation leading to the rooms that would always hold a place of terror in Cole's memory. He tried not to look, but the battery-operated floodlights that had been set up drew his attention. Men in uniforms swarmed the interior. He looked away.

A few more steps and they were approaching Daniel's body. Thankfully, he was covered with a sheet. They skirted by silently.

In the basement hallway, Cole noticed some folks cleaning up the shock treatment room. One of them was Dr. Slaver. The doctor glanced up and noticed Cole, but quickly returned his attention to the work at hand. Cole could've sworn that he looked embarrassed. He also had a bandage on the bridge of his nose.

When they reached the first floor, the first thing Cole noticed was the activity. People were coming and going through the main entrance. The lady at the reception desk who'd been there when he arrived was back at her post. She was calmly answering phones and shuffling papers at the same time. Cole found it surprising that the phones worked and even more surprised that the lady wasn't frantic with all the commotion going on around her.

Nurse Stern gently took his arm and guided him to the side, away from the activity. Unlike the receptionist, she looked frazzled. Her entire world had been destroyed in a manner of minutes.

"Cole," she said, and looked from side to side.

"What?" This was strange.

"You were talking to Lambert."

"Yeah. So?" he whispered.

"I don't know how to tell you this except just to say it. Lambert died right before I came down to the tunnel. I'm sorry. I know you liked him."

Hold on a second. That meant Lambert was already dead when they were talking in the tunnel. But just a short while before, he seemed to be doing okay when he warned him and Kenny about going outside with all the violent men on the loose. Could someone die that quickly?

"He just keeled over, probably a heart attack. He's had some recent heart problems. The storm might've been too much for him."

Cole guessed it could happen that fast after all. He suddenly felt very tired. The pain was getting worse. But he wasn't as upset about Lambert as he would've expected. Lambert was probably a lot happier wherever he was now.

"You didn't see him, then. With me in the tunnel."

Nurse Stern shook her head. "No. I just heard you say goodbye to him."

Nurse Stern babbled on about something more, but he never heard it. His ears, mind, and everything else were fading fast. They walked to the main door and met Roy as he came up the front steps to collect Cole.

20
Requiem

THE SMALL GIFT SHOP WAS in the lobby area. T-shirts flew off the makeshift shelves along with a couple of mugs. They made a killing as usual, and Rutledge loved them for it. Rutledge had already started talking about hiring part-timers to staff the thing—students and bored housewives who wanted to get out of the house for a while. The sale of overpriced stuff was an added boon, and merchandise with the asylum's name was getting out there. He attributed it to Evie and Chaz's enthusiastic tours. Chaz never contradicted him on that point.

Individual parties poked around for a little bit afterward, but most left pretty quickly. The trio of couples could be heard outside on the main steps. They were on their way back to the inn. The college girls were chatting in the lobby about additional plans for the evening, and as soon as they noticed they were alone, they dashed out with an apology. Which was unnecessary. Rutledge had no problem with people hanging around for a bit.

"The older guy is still on the second floor," Evie informed him.

Chaz's confusion must've shown on his face because she added, "He asked if he could go upstairs and take a picture."

Normally, customers weren't allowed to wander off unaccompanied because there were so many hallways and nooks and crannies where they could get lost. However, the second-floor access was just up the main staircase and within eyeshot of the lobby.

"No problem. I'll go tell him we're gonna be closing up shop."

Chaz bounded up the steps two at a time. Things were good. The tour had gone well, and he and Evie were connecting. He wasn't sure how all of this was going to play out in the long run, including the job, but he could live with ambiguity right now.

He scampered to the second floor and made his way to the propped door of the pediatric ward. Yep, there was the old dude, standing in the common room.

With minor irritation, Chaz noticed that he had turned on the digital frame and paused the slideshow. The picture on the screen was of the three boys taken by the journalist in the early sixties. The old dude stood transfixed before the frame and didn't turn when Chaz entered the ward. His hands were behind his back, clasping a cell phone.

"Sorry, sir. We need to start closing up."

The old dude remained still. "I remember the day this was taken."

Chaz stopped dead in his tracks. "I'm sorry?" he whispered.

"Ah," the old dude said as he made a quarter turn and looked at Chaz. "I remember when they took this picture. It was right before Timmy died."

Chaz felt his heartbeat in his ears. He'd heard what the guy said, but it made no sense. His brain was working overtime trying to get his head around it. All he could come up with was, "You were there?"

"There?" The Old Dude smiled. It was kind but sad at the same time. "Yes, I was there. That's me on the left."

Chaz stepped forward and peered at the photo as if for the first time. The guy was referring to the youngest of the boys, the one who had taken off his shirt and tucked it into the back of his pants.

Chaz wanted to turn and yell for Evie to come hear this, but he didn't need to. She had just strolled into the room with a stunned expression. She'd obviously heard. Still, Chaz couldn't help bringing her up to speed.

"That's him on the left."

Evie could only nod.

"I enjoyed your tour. I never in a million years expected to see this picture. In fact, I had forgotten all about it. I had to take my own photo."

Chaz's head bobbled up and down. "That's okay. Um, can you, um…"

"Prove it? I don't know. Probably not. I can tell you where your information is incorrect if that'll help. Maybe it'll help future tours."

"Um, sure." Chaz couldn't think of anything else to say.

"Definitely," Evie said. "Like what?"

"Well, for starters, that impressive clip of the girl kneeling and then getting up from the common room floor." He looked at them for acknowledgement. Chaz held out his hand as if to say "go on."

"That's from the second floor. This common room. Not the one on the womens' ward. The girl was a girl, not a young woman. She was around fourteen, and her name was Cynthia. She committed suicide after Timmy died. She was a cutter before cutting was in. There were scars on her face. A hell of a place for her to commit self-injury."

The old man turned and looked back at the photo in the frame. "That's Timmy with the football. You're right. He did enjoy sports and was a phenomenal athlete. Although you wouldn't know it by looking at him."

"How'd he die?" Evie asked. Her voice was soft, compassionate.

"From what I gather it was a massive cerebral hemorrhage which happened during or shortly after an electroconvulsive session. It's hard to imagine how the two couldn't be related, but evidently there's no causal relationship. A brain bleed is not a side effect of ECT."

The old man walked to the point where he could see straight in to the boys' dormitory down the hall. "My bed was the last one. You can see it from here."

Chaz recalled seeing him touching the mattress and running his hand across the head of the bedframe during the tour.

"The bed next to mine was Kenny's. He's the strapping young man in the middle." He referred again to the picture of the three boys.

Three real boys with very real lives and all that went with it. Chaz hadn't given it much thought until now. He felt suddenly ashamed.

"It's funny. When you're kids and you're in a place like this, you don't think of each other as mentally ill. At least I didn't. Looking back at it, I suppose Cynthia had bipolar disorder. I didn't know her long, but there were mood swings and the scars of her previous self-injuries. Maybe she had suicidal ideation or attempts in her past. Who knows? I can tell you that I made great friends here. And saw horrifying things that forever haunted every part of my existence."

Dusk was setting in and the shadows were lengthening within the room. Chaz looked for a place to sit and thought the best place would be the dining room. He motioned in that direction.

"Would you like to hear the facts?"

"Please," Chaz said.

"Then let's sit." Old Dude strolled to one of the chairs, pulled it out from the table, and waited for Evie.

Evie murmured a thank you and sat. Chaz moved swiftly to a light switch, turned it on, and also sat. The old man was last.

He cleared his throat. "By the way, I'm Twilight Eyes. At least I think I am based on your tale. Hell of a name to be stuck with, though."

Chaz thought he was going to shit his pants.

The old man told his version of the events. Chaz wished he had an audio recorder. Or at least a pen and a pad of paper. Evie was probably thinking the same.

In addition to finding out about Cynthia and Timmy, this is what they learned:

The reason why the two jumpers fell to their deaths.

That Twilight Eyes—the old man—was a seer (and what that meant).

Daniel the handyman was not a killer, but a kind man who treated them like they were everyday kids.

The Creeper was real and a nurse named Dale was the Creeper. And he did ghastly things.

Some staff were child predators.

There was no patient revolt but a tornado that created chaos on that particular day—probably the very tornado they had referred to earlier in the tour.

Twilight Eyes and another boy survived the clutches of the Creeper in a two-room nightmare midway down the Dead Tunnel.

Chaz was working to keep the man's version of events straight in his memory. One thing stood out. The man's description of the two rooms in the Dead Tunnel was dead-on. So the dude was telling the truth. He'd been in those rooms once, when he'd first heard about the patient killing two staff members. He wondered why that was the version of the story that survived.

"The police officer who gave me a ride away from this place was named Roy. He was undercover here as a nurse's aide. Law enforcement had an idea that something strange was going on as people connected to the place went missing. Anyway, in the car on our way to town, he said to give him a call if I needed anything. He told me his name, Roy Kennedy. 'Like the president,' he said. That was easy to remember. I did seek his help not too long after."

A million questions were ricocheting in Chaz's mind. The best he could come up with was, "What's your name?"

The man smiled. He took reached into his back pocket and removed his wallet. From the wallet he produced a business card.

Cole Nightshade.

Cole…Coal…Twilight. All words indicating something dark. The explanation for how the name Twilight Eyes came into being?

"Why'd you come back?"

"I heard you were open for business. I was in DC for a funeral and made a detour on the way home. The boy in the middle of your picture passed away."

"Kenny? He died?" Evie sounded crushed. Chaz felt that way too.

"Sadly, yes. Cancer. Came on quickly and took him even faster."

"So, you stayed friends all these years?"

The old man—no, it was Cole Nightshade now—sat back in this chair. "I didn't see him again until seven years later. In Vietnam, of all places. I remember him saying, 'We only see each other in shitstorms.' He was a higher rank than me. We ended up on a mission of sorts over there. Combat that nobody could've anticipated. After the war we acquired quite a bit of formal education, entered similar occupations, and worked together on numerous occasions. Never saw that happening when I was here."

The asylum was peacefully quiet. There was nothing menacing or threatening in the air. The realization that people had survived this place and went on to live productive lives hit Chaz with stunning clarity. He'd never really considered the afterwards part of the individuals' tales.

Nightshade stood. "Sorry, you two. I'm beat."

"We'll walk you out," Evie said.

All three walked down the stairs together and into the lobby. Once there, Chaz lagged behind frantically and worked his smartphone. He found what he was looking for.

This wasn't just an obituary but an entire freaking article. Kenny, or Kenneth in the story, was some hotshot.

Chaz scanned his phone, swiping through the text. Words

flashed by. Federal agent...federal agency positions...presidential appointments...military service. There was more, but the words melted before his eyes.

Chaz looked up. Nightshade and Evie pulled away in front of him. "My God," he whispered. He continued reading. Eulogy offered by childhood friend Cole Nightshade, *both orphans...military...federal agent...*

"My God. Holy shit."

Evie turned around and stared. Had he spoken aloud? Chaz scrambled to catch up.

"I'm staying at the inn on the grounds this evening. I'm leaving around ten tomorrow morning. Feel free to contact me if you have any questions."

Chaz couldn't believe it. "You can count on it. Thank you so much. I'll be up all night preparing questions and recording notes."

They escorted Nightshade to the front door.

"Mr. Nightshade," Evie said as they stepped outside. "I really appreciate this, but why are you doing this? I mean, this is a nothing thing."

Nightshade smiled. "No, Evie. This is not 'nothing.' People died here. Kids died here. Facts are important. Truth is important. We no longer have facts or truth in this country and that's a damn shame."

Nightshade took a step and then halted. He cocked his head, and Chaz wondered if there was a problem.

"Pardon me, please." He wedged between Chaz and Evie and returned to the lobby. Evie rushed first to catch up. Chaz was on her heels.

Nightshade stood at the bottom of the stairs looking up to the second floor. Evie gasped. Chaz couldn't make a sound. Chills ran down his spine.

The kickball was floating in midair at the top of the stairs, not far from the door to the pediatric ward.

The ball spun as if rotating on an extended index finger. An index finger that nobody could see.

Nightshade stared at the ball. He smiled and nodded. "Goodbye, Timmy."

The ball flew toward them as if tossed underhand. Its flight was gentle.

Nightshade caught it easily.

"I believe this is yours." He offered the ball to Chaz, walked by himself to the front door, and left.

About the Author

ANTHONY HAINS IS A PROFESSOR emeritus of counseling psychology with a specialization in pediatric psychology. He retired in May 2018 after thirty-one years at the University of Wisconsin–Milwaukee. He is the author of *Sleep in the Dust of the Earth*, *The Torment*, *Sweet Aswang*, *The Disembodied*, *Dead Works*, and *Birth Offering*. Anthony lives with his wife in Whitefish Bay, Wisconsin. They have one daughter.

Made in the USA
Monee, IL
01 May 2020

28955872R00150